The Asthmatic Kid
and Other Stories

THE ASTHMATIC KID
AND OTHER STORIES

Mark Tulin

Lake Dallas, Texas

Copyright © 2020 by Mark Tulin
All rights reserved
Printed in the United States of America

FIRST EDITION

The Asthmatic Kid and Other Stories is a work of fiction. Names, characters, places, and incidents either are the products of the author's imagination or are used fictitiously. Any resemblance to actual events, locales, businesses, companies, or persons, living or dead, is entirely coincidental.

Requests for permission to reprint material from this work should be sent to:

> Permissions
> Madville Publishing
> P.O. Box 358
> Lake Dallas, TX 75065

ACKNOWLEDGMENTS
Grateful acknowledgment is made to the editors of the following journals, magazines, and podcasts where these stories first appeared: "Crazy Grandpa" in *Creative Writers Outloud Podcast*; "Weekend in Chelsea", "The Street of My Childhood" and "The Psychedelic Basement" on *Fiction on the Web*; "Room Full of Strangers" on *Smokebox.net*; "Under the Suburban Sky" (Originally titled "Weekend in the Suburbs") and "The Spirit of the Wooden Box" in *The Cabinet of Heed*; "Dark Clouds Over Baseball" in *eFiction*; "Finding My Father" in *Dual Coast Magazine*; "To Princess Lily" in *White Ash Literary Magazine (Thriving)*; "Santiago on Percussion" in *Page & Spine*.

Author photo: Erica Urech
All other photos provided by Mark Tulin from his family photo collection.

ISBN: 978-1-948692-46-5 paperback, 978-1-948692-47-2 ebook
Library of Congress Control Number: 2020936685

*for my parents
who allowed me the freedom to explore.*

Contents

The Asthmatic Kid 1

Crazy Grandpa 65

Hazleton by Noon 74

Under the Suburban Sky 79

Dark Clouds Over Baseball 87

Weekend in Chelsea 95

The Psychedelic Basement 103

Santiago on Percussion 110

Mrs. Lindy's Boarding House 116

Room Full of Strangers 123

The Street of My Childhood 130

To Princess Lilly 136

Fall So Beautifully 140

The Spirit of the Wooden Box 145

Finding My Father 148

About the Author 153

The Asthmatic Kid

It was common knowledge that my Dad slept with a whole lot of slutty women. My Uncle Leo was no angel, either. He didn't have a sober day in his life, and he probably bedded far worse whores than my father. What's more, he made life miserable for Aunt Mary, giving her stomach ulcers and making her fat with worry. Then there was my crazy Grandpa Izzy.

Although Grandpa wasn't a whoremaster, he was a raging alcoholic and a pugilist; he'd drink any bottle wrapped in a paper bag and fight anyone who looked at him sideways. And who knows how many alcoholic forefathers there were in Leningrad and Moscow that tarnished my name.

Sitting on this cold-assed cement step unable to breathe, I was paying the price for the crimes of my family. Unable to move, I foolishly stared directly into the winter sun, imploring its warming powers to heal my current troubles in one shining moment. Despite my lame pleas to the sun gods, I shivered like a hairless Chihuahua, abandoned and remorseful.

I took puffs of my emergency inhaler for Dad's adultery, a few for Uncle Leo's alcoholism, and more for the rest of my forefathers for all the mischief they probably did in Old Russia. And there's my insane mother. How pathetic she was. She suffered mentally for whatever sins her family committed ten times over. Her Dad was doomed before he even got started. He died when my mother was only nine. He fell onto a rat-infested New York City train track, pushed or jumped—who knows for sure.

All we knew was that a train hit him—a human roadkill. My mother's life changed right on the spot.

I've come to realize that a family is like a religious belief. The more you worship and believe in them, the more dysfunctional they will become. The more you idolize and praise your family members for the things you think they are doing for you, the less likely you'll find any peace in your life.

Enough of this rambling, I'm beginning to sound like my mother. Too much thinking about things I can't change. Have to cough up the phlegm (which could be my family) that's suffocating my airways. This asthma clouds my mind like a toxic gas storm. It makes me dizzy with the past, and I can't think straight in the present. If only I could breathe. If only I could cry. I wet my parched lips with my tongue. My throat feels like the texture of sandpaper.

It's hard not to assume that my predicament wasn't due to my family, especially my parents. They fought a lot when I was a baby and a toddler. I vaguely remember making myself wheeze and choke to get them to stop yelling or slapping each other, and to focus on me, their baby. One night, I thought my mother bit off my Dad's penis during a late-night bedroom fight. I heard him scream and curse while she gave him a sinister laugh. I just wanted all of it to stop. My efforts to detour them from their insanity with my asthma had failed. They blamed each other for my crying and two shitty lungs. From an early age, I realized that I was doomed.

I was four or five. My parents had another one of those stupid shouting matches, and before I knew it, I got entangled in their war. They pulled me in different directions. My Mom had one arm and my Dad the other. It was crazy, an innocent little child ripped in half. Dad called her a "bitch," and Mom called him a "bastard." Mom yanked me out of Dad's grasp and ran down the steps into the basement with my little legs trying to keep pace. I didn't know where she was headed. Then, before I knew it, the glass door crashed on my face. I screamed at the top of my lungs.

You'd think this would quiet them down. Nope.

My father shouted: "See what the fuck you did, Lil?"

The blood poured out of my forehead like a broken faucet. My parents kept yelling and blaming each other in the car ride to Einstein Hospital.

A shard of glass right above my eyebrow was removed. It could have hit my eye. Then I would have been blind the rest of my life. Even at four, I knew I was screwed.

2

My Dad would say, "Stop blaming others and take responsibility for your actions." He pointed out that I was the one who fucked up my life, not him or Mom. "You broke into that synagogue through a window and climbed down the basketball stanchion," he reminded me. Yes, that's true. Bergman, Padidas, and I turned on the lights and played roughhouse and twenty-one. I knew I was committing a petty crime, but I didn't care. I was a kid. Kids have a right to break the rules and do whatever they want if they aren't hurting anyone.

Stuck on the step with only my asthma to keep me company, I felt guilty for every little thing in my life. I believed that God punished me for breaking into the temple, drinking a 32-ounce bottle of cheap orange soda, and eating those delicious chocolate éclairs. At the time, I felt that the synagogue was probably going to use the food for the High Holidays. Why not celebrate the holidays sooner with my friends included? Wasn't I entitled to have some fun?

Besides, my Jewish brothers and sisters had never done anything for me in my fourteen years on earth except give me a bar mitzvah, a bar mitzvah that I never wanted in the first place, and would have never gotten if my Grandma didn't orchestrate it. What are a few minutes of basketball and a couple of chocolate éclairs for an asthmatic kid, anyway?

"Hey, you!" the security guard screamed. His voice caught

us by surprise. He had a black patch over his right eye like he was a pirate. We dropped everything. He chased us like a speed racer and caught me by the scruff of my neck, tackled me to the ground, and called me a *puny little sonovabitch*. I didn't mind the sonovabitch part, but puny felt insulting.

"I'm taking you thieving shits to the rabbi's office. You're in hot water now."

"Stop hurting me!" I screamed at the security guard who was twisting my ear into a pretzel. Bergman and Padidas were as scared as I'd ever seen and sat right down without any resistance in the rabbi's office. They looked like a couple of whipped dorks.

I knew the rabbi from my bar mitzvah. He didn't have the beard, and he didn't look like such a mean asshole. He was kind to me then. He saw that I was nervous about speaking in front of people and only gave me one line of Hebrew to recite.

"Just read this single line, Harry. That's all you have to do. I'll do the rest."

I thought he was my friend and cared. But now he acted like he didn't even know me. It must have been all the weight he gained and that neckbeard that made him appear more like a bear than a religious figure.

My plan was to act the way Bergman and Padidas were doing and make-believe I felt terrible about breaking into his precious synagogue, eating those chocolate éclairs, and drinking orange soda that was so flat that it made me nauseous.

"I'm sorry," I said trying to break the tension, "but those chocolate éclairs were badass. Where did you get them?"

He stared at me with his bushy eyebrows pinched together. He was like the Wizard of Oz of the Jews, only not as mysterious and entertaining. He didn't hide behind a screen like the Oz or talk through a microphone, but he hid behind his advanced degrees and his pompous status in the Jewish community—while I was a lowly, little squirt in his eyes. To him, I was just a bad kid, and would probably never amount to much. I'd end up as one of the unfortunate Jews with a lousy career and a bleak future. He probably thought I'd marry a *shiksa* and live in a dumpy house full of blond-haired, blue-eyed dirty babies—a disgrace to the tribe.

He tried to intimidate us with big words. When he spoke, his nostrils flared. After each drag from his pipe, smoke poured out of his nose like a snarling bull. He sat behind a mahogany desk in his paneled office, looked me in the eye, and then glared at Bergman and Padidas as if he was going to hypnotize us into being good, obedient children.

"I'm not going to be easy on you," he said. His jaw moved sideways when he talked, and I could hear the gnashing of his teeth when he didn't. His head was mainly skull because he had only a sparse tuft of gray hair plastered down. The veins in his forehead pulsated like water coursing through an old garden hose. And then the guy pulled the Jew card.

"How could a Jew do such a thing?" And he looked at us with a scowl, like little pieces of rancid gefilte fish, worthless and uneatable. "The *goyim*, I could understand—they don't know any better. *But a Jew?* To do this to your own people is unforgivable. I'm speechless."

I wish he were speechless because he pissed me off. Playing basketball and eating chocolate éclairs wasn't an anti-Semitic thing. It was a dumb kid thing, that's all. We weren't disrespecting a Jewish institution, but were playing an innocent game of *twenty-one,* for Chrissake.

My asthma kicked in when he laid the guilt trip on us. My chest tightened like someone was turning a vice. No one could hear my lungs' rattling like they were on loudspeakers. When the rabbi spoke, I heard a symphony of wheezy lungs, like violins and cellos out of tune, clashing sounds ringing in my ears. I wanted to cough up a big loogie the size of Texas right between his eyes. Instead, I just imagined it.

"I have to tell your parents about this," he said, pausing to stare me down. He dialed his black, rotary phone after I reluctantly gave him my number. My mother picked up, which was perfect. She wasn't good for much, but talking to a guy like Rabbi Drumsky was ideal.

I could see the stupid expression of annoyance on his face when he spoke to my Mom. He knew right off the bat that she was a loony bag. He lost all of his power when he talked to her, castrated right on the spot. His penis was dangling by a thread. His college diplomas were useless when my mother was on the phone. He was just another lost and pathetic soul trying to harass my Mom. After a few minutes, his face became gaunt and wrinkled. His complexion was as red as a traffic light. My mother reduced this big imposing guy into a mouse.

I was so happy to see him being tortured by my mother's insanity that it almost made me cry. Now he knew what trauma I went through every day. He kept responding, "Okay. Okay, Mrs. Tobin. I understand. You don't need to worry. I'll take care of everything. Now, please, Mrs. Tobin, calm down. Everything will be fine." I don't know what she said, but there was a loose pile of chicken livers sitting in the chair in front of me.

He handed me the phone like he was getting rid of some disgusting venereal disease.

"Harry!" my mother screamed into the receiver. "Listen to the man. He's a rabbi, for Chrissake. Maybe he'll help you get a job in the *shul*. Ask him if you could work in the bookstore."

I handed the phone back to the rabbi, who was much relieved to hang up. His hands quivered, and his red forehead poured sweat. "Don't worry," he said. "I won't call the police this time. You're getting off real lucky, I can tell you that much."

To save his reputation, he gave us a long, rambling lecture that felt like a funeral sermon and, I'm sure, far worse than being locked up by the police.

"The next time you boys deface this house of worship, I'm going to call the police and press charges to the full extent of the law. Don't you know that our synagogue was victimized by anti-Semites last month?"

"Alright, already," I muttered to myself. "Give me ten-thousand points of bad karma and send me the hell home."

Sure, I got shaken after all that. I nearly pissed in my pants and threw up the éclairs. For a while, I vowed to God that I would never break into a synagogue again. I would be an angel and live by the Ten Commandments and never do anything that would hurt anyone's feelings or break anybody's rules. My fear wore off after a few days like a bad cold, and I was back to normal: A wheezy, congested, and undersized kid with balls.

3

I didn't know why all these painful memories came to me while I was having an asthma attack. It's sad enough to sit on the cold step and cough up ugly-colored phlegm, but thinking about all my misdeeds and failed adventures seemed to make my asthma worse. Some doctor once told me that I needed to go right to the hospital as soon as blood appeared in my mucus, but for now, I just wanted to get my cold ass off the step and be able to breathe again.

Of course, I had to sit on the stoop and think about the schoolyard fight with fuckface Radberg. It was in the middle of May, near the end of the school year, about 4:30 p.m. on a Friday. I stood in the center of the large yellow circle at the Moreton schoolyard, where they played dodgeball during gym class. But that day I was going to be in a fistfight or at least that's what everyone expected.

I was the first to arrive. I wanted to get it over quickly so I could go home and watch *The Three Stooges* on TV. Maybe I could say something scary to Radberg like I choked a kid once with my bare hands. But it was Radberg who had the big hands. I saw his father once. He was built like an ape and must have been six-foot-five. Right now, Radberg's only a couple of inches taller than me, but in a few years, he's going to grow like his crazy-ape father and kick my ass ten times over.

The idiot challenged me to a fight after school because I kept bullying him for money during recess. He said that he wasn't going to take my shit anymore. "Come on, *dickbrain*,"

I said, acting tough in front of everyone, especially the girls. "You're not going to fight me. You're too *chickenshit*."

Well, I pushed the wrong kid. He looked me straight in the eye and wasn't scared one bit like the rest of the kids I shoved around. "Meet me at the Moreton Circle at 4:30," he said. "I'm going to take care of you once and for all."

So, there I was in the barren schoolyard. I didn't want to be there in the first place and considered not showing up, but I didn't want people to think I was a coward. I sat in the middle of the blacktop schoolyard in my cut-off jeans and Converse Chuck Taylors. I kept picking the rubber rim of my sneaker until it came off and pulled it like Turkish taffy just to occupy myself. There was a scab on my right leg that I got from scraping my knee on the sidewalk. I could feel my nose gurgling and dripping from the allergies in the humid air. It was probably ragweed, I concluded, based on what my allergist might say. I wiped my nose with a rolled-up tissue that had been in my pocket for ages because I was too lazy to get a new one.

I stared at the basketball hoops without nets to my left, where I labored through a full-court pick-up game earlier that day with some Puerto Rican and black kids. I'd much rather be playing with them than waiting for Radberg. It's funny, I don't even think I hit anyone before. I felt like punching my mother a few times and pounding my chest when it got tight, but honestly, I've never thrown a punch in my life. I worried that Radberg knew deep down inside I was a fraud. Padidas once told me that if you act soft, kids will pick on you. Half the guys who I bully could probably kick my ass if they only knew that I was a pussy.

I waited in the middle of the schoolyard like an abandoned child. I didn't want to jump up and down to get warmed up because I was afraid it might aggravate my asthma. Instead, I sat and waited, thinking I would somehow weasel out of this fight. A cool breeze blew on my bare legs that sent chills up and down my spine. I hoped I wasn't coming down with something.

4

Mrs. Barnett, my fifth-grade teacher, said it was a miracle that I didn't have psychological problems given who my parents were. My Mom was crazier than any mother I knew, and my Dad enjoyed banging any woman with a big rack no matter how ugly. The truth was, even though my Mom was bonkers, I never knew her to be any other way. And my father wasn't all bad, despite his propensity for big boobs and being pissed off for marrying my mother.

"Harry, you're an underachiever," Mrs. Barnett told me whenever I got a poor grade on a test. She was a short black woman with a severe handicap and a big toothy smile. She was all twisted, walked with a pair of crutches, and said that she had juvenile arthritis since she was a little girl. I didn't like most teachers, but I found her to be genuine. I was impressed by her enthusiasm and helping kids like me even though her body was gnarled beyond repair. She thought I was a lot smarter than I acted. I thought I was who I was and whether I was smart or dumb, it didn't matter. I didn't give two shits about school or doing what I was supposed to, according to what other people thought.

"You're the only teacher I respect, Mrs. Barnett," I once said. "I wish you weren't so crippled. It kills me to watch you walk."

"I'm used to it by now, Harry. But I wish you would take care of yourself instead of worrying about me. Try taking your books home, doing your assignments, and staying out trouble. You've got a lot to offer. If only you could see it."

No matter how many words of encouragement Mrs. Barnett gave me, school was never going to be my bag. It was a drag lugging around heavy textbooks and worrying about homework or what crappy assignments I had to turn in. I was much more comfortable playing sports in the afternoon, coming home when it got dark, and feeding my face with corned beef sandwiches or leftover pizza from Dante's Inferno. I worried about my jump shot and whether my batting stance was wide enough, not some stupid math quiz.

5

What was I thinking? Oh yeah, the schoolyard fight. At about 4:40 p.m., Radberg and his friends entered the gate at Summerland Avenue. Once they saw me sitting in the middle of the yellow circle, I jumped up and began to demonstrate my fancy footwork like Cassius Clay getting ready to pound Sonny Liston. I wanted to trick Radberg into believing that I've done this before and that it's just another fight for me. I'll kick his ass as easy as eating a bag of Wise Potato Chips. I remembered a match I saw on TV where this guy punched another fighter so hard in the stomach that his frickin' teeth flew out of his mouth. That's what I imagined doing to Radberg. I wanted to get a quick punch in, a sucker punch to the belly, and watch his teeth fly out of his mouth, braces and everything. Then the kids would make me some kind of folk hero, like David kicking the shit out of Goliath and then chopping off his head to show everybody how bad he was.

I never hit a kid in my life, so I wouldn't have enough balls to chop off Radberg's head. I was afraid that if I hit someone in the face or the chest, they might get seriously hurt, and I'd end up in prison for murder. My father once said, "Use your mind, not your brawn." He knew someone who hit a guy in the solar plexus that left him dead right on the spot. I didn't know if it was bullshit, but my Dad seemed to be convincing enough.

Radberg stood about six feet from me in the circle. He wore a pair of white Jack Purcell's, Levi's, and a gray and blue striped polo. He didn't say a word but balled up his right hand like he was ready to let it fly. I kept staring at those freakishly wide knuckles of his. He was the best damn handball player in our grade and could hit a pinkie over the schoolyard fence for a homer, whereas I could barely punch it past the infielders for a single. I cringed at the thought of those large ugly knuckles entering my mouth and breaking my teeth into tiny pieces. My teeth were already yellow and crooked. I didn't want them to look any worse.

I was determined, though. I didn't want to have Padidas and Bergman find out that I was a punk and couldn't handle myself.

"Are you sure you want to do this?" I asked Radberg in a friendly but manly voice.

"Uh, duh," he stuttered, caught off guard. He didn't trust me for a second and thought that my friendly demeanor was a ruse. He continued to hold up his balled fist in case I came after him with a flurry of punches.

I danced around, surprising him with my boxing moves, bouncing on my tiptoes, and throwing short jabs in the air at invisible jaws. I wanted him to think that I had serious boxing skills and that I meant business. I knew how to imitate a boxer, even if my legs were skinny and my arms had no muscle tone. The more I jumped around, the more difficult it was for me to breathe. It was pollen and ragweed season, and I knew that the longer that I exerted myself in the humid, windblown air, the more challenging it would be to keep this charade going.

"What's this shit?" Radberg finally asked, annoyed at my dancing routine. He was getting dizzy, turning in circles following my every movement. He pointed at me and rolled his eyes to his dorky friends who just shrugged their shoulders and kept looking at my dance as if they were watching one of the guys on *American Bandstand*.

"Are you sure you want to fight?" I asked.

Since he didn't answer right away, I explained with a straight face that I once hit a sixth-grader so hard in the ribs that his guts spilled out. "They had to scoop it up with a shovel." And, trying to make it more realistic, I motioned to the end of the schoolyard by the water fountain where that imaginary event took place. "If you look hard enough," I added, "you could still see the bloodstain."

I could lie through my teeth with a straight face, and people would buy into it. Padidas once said that lying is the art of selling yourself, and if you're a good liar, you'll be more popular, especially with the girls.

I bounced around Radberg like crazy. I got winded fast and

could feel my lungs struggling for each breath, fearing that I could collapse at any moment. Then I'd have to reach into my pocket for the emergency inhaler, revealing my hidden weakness.

"Do we really want to fight?" I asked again.

I kept moving around him and throwing jabs and right hooks. I didn't want to stop and be an easy target for his big knuckles. I could see I was wearing him down mentally. It would just take a little more time.

Then I did something gutsy. I moved a couple of feet closer, foamed at the mouth with saliva, and flailed my arms in manic fashion like I had rabies and was going to obliterate Radberg completely.

I must have scared the kid something awful, because he backed up and had a worried look on his face like he was about to be pounced on by a German Shepherd.

"Whatever you want to do," he finally relented. By then, the clouds had moved in, and it was getting dark. I assumed that he was hungry or wanted to get home before the rain. I knew kids like Radberg. He might have big knuckles, but he was a pussy at heart, just like me. Only I was better at hiding it.

I stopped bouncing around and coughed a couple of times, feeling the phlegm rise to my throat. I reached out my hand, and he reluctantly shook it. I breathed a sigh of relief, for I narrowly avoided a major ass-kicking.

"Don't worry," I assured him. "I'm not going to mess with you anymore. From now on, you're cool with me."

I almost added, "That's if you give me your lunch money every day," but I held back and just coughed and spit. When Radberg and his friends left the schoolyard, I quickly gave myself two squirts of the emergency inhaler.

6

Of course, I had to take a piss. I squeezed my sphincters as hard as I could, trying to keep myself from wetting my pants. But my ass was so cold and numb from the icy cement steps that before I knew it, something warm and wet ran down my leg, forming a puddle at my feet.

Peeing in my pants brought me back to those years that I'd soon like to forget. It occurred during the most vulnerable time in my life, before adolescence. My Aunt was bothered by it the most. She woke me up in the middle of the night to go to the bathroom and prevented me from drinking any liquids after 6 p.m., even if I was thirsty from eating pretzels. I tried to listen to Aunt Mary—use the bathroom before I went to bed, stop drinking liquids, and get up in the middle of the night if I felt like peeing.

Nothing seemed to work.

I felt guilty for something that I couldn't control, and the people around me either were angry or thought it was a joke.

Once I realized I had wet the bed in the morning, I put an empty drinking glass where the damp spot was and hoped that Aunt Mary would believe that it was spilled water. But once she smelled the soaked sheets, she knew the empty glass was a ruse.

"Who are you fooling?" she asked in an irritable tone.

"Myself, I guess."

She put on plastic gloves and shook her head. She desperately wanted this phase in my life to be over so I could be a normal kid. She was tired of washing wet stinky sheets every day when she could do something better with her time.

I remember those mornings that I had helped Jake and Roy (my Uncle's employees) unload the produce truck in front of the house. I looked up and was mortified to see Aunt Mary hanging wet sheets off the second-floor balcony. The guys knew that the urine-soaked sheets were mine. They could smell it from where they were standing, saw the big yellow stain in plain view, and let me have it.

"Pass the watermelon, piss-the-bed," said Jake laughing like an idiot.

"Pee-the-pants," said his brother Roy and would make believe he was holding his privates.

I wanted to disappear, but there was nowhere to go. It felt like a knife to the belly that just kept bleeding. My reputation as a cool kid from Philly ruined. I felt like crying, but I decided to laugh at myself instead. "It keeps me warm at night," I told them and gave the biggest smile like it was no big deal, that I was still a cool kid despite not being able to control my bladder at night.

"Try using a warm blanket next time; it's a lot dryer," said Jake while Roy kept pulling his zipper up and down.

I understood Aunt Mary's frustration. She was tired of keeping my bed dry. She hated to pick up urine-soaked sheets every morning from a kid she expected great things from. She kept saying, "You're not a baby, Harry. You're not a baby anymore."

"I know," I said, shrugging my shoulders, not knowing what else to say. I just looked like a sad puppy and hoped to be forgiven.

7

I could feel the pee soaking my white sweat socks and accumulating in my Converse, leaking out through the air holes. You'd think that someone would come outside by now and ask what's going on. *Why are you all wet with piss, boy?* You'd think they'd notice a little kid in agony with his face turning blue, hands frostbitten from the cold. But no, people really didn't give a shit. People had their blinds closed and lived like hermits in Philly, and whatever horrifying stuff happened outside their doors was no concern of theirs.

Maybe the people in the house could sense that I was not only a bully but also a thief, and who wants to help someone like that?

I must have taken after my Dad, who stole produce from a couple of creeps and sold it in his store like nothing was wrong. And Grandma swiped hard candies from Penn Fruit and said that since everybody does it, it must be all right. Grandma also stole silverware and breadbaskets from restaurants, pens and notepads from banks, and who knows what else she took that I missed.

But it was Bergman and Padidas who taught me everything I knew about thievery. They were three years older and had much more street smarts than I did. They knew how to smoke cigarettes without coughing, how to use condoms even if they didn't have sex, and how to steal anything without looking suspicious. They were the epitome of cool and all I had to do was copy their style, and I'd be sitting pretty.

Padidas, who had a big gut like his father, had thick curly hair, two eyebrows that came together as one, and could throw a hardball through a brick wall.

"We need to get new baseball equipment because this stuff isn't worth crap," he said.

"Yeah," I agreed. "That would be cool."

Bergman agreed, too. "I could use a heavier bat. The bats we use are for babies. It's like swinging a toothpick."

We thought about it for a couple of minutes, and then I asked Padidas, "Where are we going to get the money to buy this shit?"

Padidas, who could come up with all the angles, said, "Why don't we steal it?"

"That seems like a lot to steal," I said. "It's not like we're swiping some candy from Woolworth's. We're talking about big sports equipment."

"Sure, we could do it easy," Padidas said, sensing my doubt with his curly head looking down at me.

Bergman nervously chimed in, "I know we can do it. Lit Brothers is a piece of cake. We just go in like we're shopping for school or something, and grab the shit like we're buying it. And instead of taking it to the register, we put it down our shirts or in our pants." I could see his bony fingers shake as he rubbed them together, not with fear but with excitement. He loved to steal.

When Bergman and Padidas agreed to swipe some sports equipment from Lit Brothers, I got excited, too. I could feel their mischievous energy. We were planning a big heist like Steve McQueen did in that movie where he stole from the bank that he owned.

But unlike McQueen, we didn't have much of a plan. We went in and just let our stealing instincts take over. I was so comfortable hocking the glove, bat, and autographed baseball that I felt like going back in and snatching some shoulder pads and football cleats and any other thing I could get my hands on. With our booty safely cradled in our arms, we casually walked out through the double-doors of the department store and into the bright sunshine, giddy with happiness.

We stacked all our shit on a bus stop bench and kept looking at it all like it was an unexplained miracle. We imagined doing this every day like clockwork and perhaps dropping out of school and making a profession out of it. We saw ourselves driving expensive Caddies and limos we bought with cash from dealerships. We talked about swiping a bunch of crap and then selling it to our friends and neighbors for a massive profit without any overhead.

As Bergman looked at all the stuff, he spoke these wise words: "Doing well in school is meaningless. It all comes down to how much you own." The ironic part was that Bergman got all A's in school and didn't think it was a big deal. I think he was bored with how easy it was.

"Yeah," said Padidas. "Having the most money is the nature of the jungle."

I was the proudest sonovabitch when I walked into the house, King of the Jungle. My mother was talking to herself in the kitchen, as usual. She spoke in code, pure gibberish. They were words that only she knew, words that even the greatest minds in the world couldn't decipher. It always irritated me that my mother was the nuttiest Mom on the block while the other kids had nice mothers who baked cookies and still made sense.

I took all the stolen merchandise to my room, dropped it on my bed, and celebrated by watching *The Three Stooges* and having a nice, thick pastrami sandwich on rye.

8

It was Monday. My father was coming down from Hazleton to pick up a load of produce at the South Philly market. Our house was just a pit stop on his way there. He only came home to wash up, grab something to eat, and sleep for a few hours. Usually, we picked up a pizza or a couple of cheesesteaks for dinner. I couldn't wait to show him all the sporting goods that I stole.

I sat on the stoop and waited for his noisy Ford truck to turn the corner. I was eager to see his shiny bald head pop out of his rig, open up his arms, and hug me with his stubby fingers. It was like when the Phillies won a doubleheader, or the Eagles beat the Cowboys on Sunday.

Killing time in front of my house, I swung a baseball bat like Tony Taylor and threw the hardball high into the air over the telephone wires and caught it with my new stolen glove. I hoped that Sandy, the girl across the street with hair down to her waist, was watching from her window. I'm sure she would have been impressed with my athletic skills.

I rarely saw my Dad since he moved upstate a couple of years ago. One day he sat me on the steps and said that he had something important to say. "I'm moving to Wilkes Barre, Harry. Your mother and I think it's for the best." I remember the lump in my throat when he said those words and how the sky grew darker all of a sudden. It felt that I would fall into a sinkhole and never be able to climb out. But as time wore on, I realized it was for the best. Mom and Dad were like oil and water; they never blended well. They fought and argued about petty things that made me crazy. It's better that Dad didn't come home that often. I could only take their fighting for a few hours and was glad when Dad left.

When I saw Dad, I wanted to tell him some good news, which wasn't typical for me. There was much more bad news to share, like getting straight D's on my report card and refusing to follow my mother's directions, which was most of the time.

I always acted like things were okay with Mom and that school was a breeze, when in reality, both Mom and school were more like tropical hurricanes.

I heard Dad downshifting his big Ford and pulling around the corner, barely avoiding bringing down several tree branches. My heart raced when I saw him navigating out of the cab and stepping down from the truck. He missed the last visit, saying there was an emergency of some sort. I didn't believe it because he pulled that excuse before. I knew he was bonking one of his sluts in Wilkes Barre. I could even picture her, not too pretty in the face but a "*helluva* rack," as Dad would say.

"The damn carburetor went," he said the moment he saw me on the steps. "Stuck on the interstate for about an hour. The transmission won't last much longer."

I could care less about his truck, but I thought I could cheer him up when I showed him my Henry Aaron glove and the Louisville Slugger, although I should have known better. All he could think about was breaking down on the interstate and being in a crappy mood. Work and his problems always took priority.

"Where did you get those?" he asked.

"Ah, I just got it s-s-somewhere. I mean, I found it."

Dad knew I was bullshitting the minute I began to stutter. He rarely saw me, but he knew me like a book.

"Do you think that I don't know you hocked this?" His face turned plum red, and I could see his blue veins pop out of his bald head. My father wasn't a big man, but he was big enough to hoist a couple of 50-pound bags of Russet potatoes over his shoulder with no problem, not even a knee buckle.

"That's all I need," he said. "I got all this crap going on. I have to deal with my truck, your mother—and now you! For Christ's sake, Harry. Why can't you do what you're supposed to do?"

A wave of shame went through me like a bad case of diarrhea as Dad tore me a new one. I wished that I had a father like Ward Cleaver who came home neat and clean, in a good mood, and if I did something wrong, he wouldn't call me a dumb sonovabitch. He might smirk a little, but he would never raise his voice or use profanity. Ward Cleaver would see me as being a foolish kid, that's all, typical growing pains for a boy my age. But instead, I sat on the stoop in front of my house about to cry. What's worse, he didn't feel hungry later on. We didn't get a pizza or a cheesesteak from Dante's Inferno like we usually did. I had to eat the dried-out Chef Boyardee ravioli that my mother had sitting on the stove for hours. Some visit with my Dad.

9

As I sat on the ice-cold step waiting for the fast-acting inhaler to work, I remembered something important about the Lit Brothers story that I forgot to mention. It happened while Dad was cursing me out on the stoop. I don't know where I got the courage, but I think I had enough of his bullshit and wanted to let him know.

"Don't be a jerkoff, Dad," I said as he was reaming me out, knowing the moment that it came out of my mouth, I was in deep shit.

Obviously, he wasn't going to stop being a jerkoff and miraculously transform into Beaver's father. He was going to be even more of a dick.

I thought for sure that Dad would hit me over the head with the Louisville Slugger and make me see stars. Instead, he spoke in a relatively calm but nasty voice, "Get the hell in the truck! We're returning this crap right now!"

As I rode in his bumpy eight-wheel truck, I imagined eating a bunch of Tastykake Coconut Juniors and growing taller than my father, as big as the Incredible Hulk. I imagined choking the sonovabitch with my giant hands until he yelled, "I give!" "What did you say? I can't hear you?" "I give. You win!"

I hated being the smallest kid in school and often fantasized about being much taller. The doctor told me that I was short because I used steroids for my asthma as a toddler and that it stunted my growth. I was a full head smaller than anyone else. It made me feel like a loser.

Something always got in the way of feeling good about myself. Besides being short, I had acne breakouts by the time I was twelve. Sometimes there were pimples on top of pimples, blackheads the size of dark eyeballs, and craters in my face after I popped them. I wanted to take Dad's straight-edged razor and shave them off. If that wasn't bad enough, I started to have thinning hair on the front part of my scalp. Imagine what was going through my mind when the wind blew? I was going to be bald just like my Dad soon. The ultimate curse!

Another thing, my voice was too high. I talked in a squeaky Mickey Mouse voice when I had to read some lame book in class. Doctor Links wrote it off to nerves, but it didn't matter what it was from, I didn't want to sound like Mickey Mouse, even though I loved Disney cartoons and watched them all the time. Mickey was a frickin' rat, for Chrisssake! I wanted girls to be all over me, not give me pieces of Swiss cheese or scream when I entered the room.

10

For much of my childhood, I felt like a dud, sitting on the stoop, watching the world go by. I'd watch people pass, mainly people I didn't know personally, but they all seemed familiar. After years of staring, everyone eventually looked like they were members of my family, like the homely guy with the long white beard. His bald head reminded me of my disheveled Uncle Leo. He walked up and down Alton Street like he was going somewhere, but he never seemed to get anywhere. Then there were the twin sisters that dressed like they were from the 1800s. They wore identical outdated clothing, uncomfortable Victorian heels, and floppy straw hats, taking each step in unison like they were in a marching band. I had to blink twice because they looked like the same person. Then there were the kids at my school. Jesse Rubinoff always tried to pick up this girl named Donna Ravine. She was the whore of the neighborhood. Donna gave anyone a blowjob that talked to her like she was a regular girl. Guys would say she looked pretty just to have sex with her. Jesse must have treated her like a slut because she wouldn't even kiss him.

Oh, shit. There were Radberg and his friends. He can't see me like this. I pulled my beanie over my head and leaned forward to tie my sneaker. Radberg had a pimple ball in his big right hand, squeezing it with those big-knuckled fingers. God, I was glad that sonovabitch didn't hit me. I'm in lousy enough shape.

As I yanked my hat above my eyes, I saw Sandy Finkle walk up the block with two of her foxy girlfriends. I wish I could get the hell up and hide behind the bush, but as soon as I tried, I felt a weight on my chest, a loud thump of a heartbeat that made me fall backward on the seat of my pants. God, I hoped she didn't see me. Christ, there's a puddle of urine that's already frozen by my feet. She's so damn cute. I loved that white parka with the furry hood that cradled her face. I wanted to hold one of her hands with the cute red mittens. I wanted to impress her, and all I could do was to stay stuck on the stoop, a helpless idiot in a pool of urine.

Oh God, she started walking toward me. She held on to the railing at the bottom of the steps. I didn't want her to get any closer and see the urine by my feet.

"What are you doing there, Harry?"

I looked up shyly. "Just waiting for a friend."

"You don't look so good. Do you want some help with anything? Should I get your mother?"

God, she was so sweet. I loved that girl. Too bad she didn't see me as a possible boyfriend. She probably looked at me as her little brother and felt sorry for my feebleness. She goes for the older guys, the guys with the thick forearms and heads of hair that will never go bald.

"No, that's okay, Sandy. I'll be fine. Just sitting here waiting for a friend, that's all. He'll be here soon. He must be in detention or something."

She turned to her friends and giggled. I watched her cute butt as she walked down the block, wishing that some miracle might bring us together. But my pathetic situation hit me like a ton of bricks.

Suddenly, I felt the urge to talk to myself, just like my mother. *Moron! Asshole! Idiot! She never speaks to you, and when she does, you have to be sitting in your piss!*

I knew I was going back into the hospital. I could sense it like a person with epilepsy who knew he was going to have a seizure. I would be a sick clown in the circus with all those medical nitwits poking and prodding me in the chest. The doctors would juggle me high up in the air like I was a bowling pin, and then make me walk a tightrope of pills, needles, and nebulizers. The nurses would make me do all kinds of acrobat crap like—sit up, lean back, turn over, open your mouth, and give me your arm. They'd stick me with long needles, hook me up to an IV and watch me walk the hallways like an invalid. The respiratory therapist would make me blow into some measuring machine really hard until the veins popped out of my head, and then they'd say it's not good enough. "You could do a better job!" they'd scream in my ear. Then they would ask me to turn over and pound my back to loosen all the phlegm like they were kneading a clump of raw dough. I imagined that my parents and friends would laugh their asses off, thinking that my misery was all a funny joke, tossing popcorn and peanuts in their mouths as the dumb clown entertained them. My suffering would lead to even more torture, which would eventually result in an early demise. My death would be the featured attraction in the center ring under the big tent. God, I hated hospitals.

11

I must have passed out on the stoop because when I woke up, I was in the back of an ambulance with a siren blaring on the way to the emergency room.

"How did I get here? Was it that lady who had her blinds closed?" I asked one of the guys in white.

"Some young girl called the police," he said. "She waited till you were safely in the ambulance, and then she left."

"A young girl?"

"Yeah, I think her name was Randy. Said she knows you."

"You mean, Sandy?"

"Yeah, I think that was it."

I felt a twinge of embarrassment and hope at the same time. *She does care about me*, I thought, as I was being hooked up to all kinds of medical crap. I wished she hadn't seen me so vulnerable and weak. I wished she hadn't been there at my absolute worst moment.

I fell asleep in the ER. I conked out dreaming of Sandy's long hair falling on my face as she kept shaking me and crying, "Are you alright, Harry? Oh, Harry—please say something? Please, don't die!"

I dreamed of her kissing me like I was some frog prince, waking me up to her beautiful brown eyes in the forest with birds circling us like a Bambi movie.

The dream ended way too soon. They transferred me to the Pulmonology Unit with a staff who'd much rather be having lunch at Burger Chef than working with a bunch of wheezy, coughing invalids.

About ten people introduced themselves to me at the same time and showed me where the plastic urinal was, just in case I couldn't get to the bathroom on time. My doctor resembled a sarcastic Don Rickles but only taller and more condescending. He was one of the snarkiest doctors I ever met, probably got a degree in it. He kept reading my medical chart and sucked his teeth like he was annoyed at me for having an asthma attack.

"When could I get out of here, Doc?" I asked impatiently.

"I think you don't know how to take care of yourself, young man. I'm not releasing you from the hospital right away in your condition."

I would have bitch-slapped him if it weren't for all the tubes and compressors that held me back.

"There seems to be a lot of damage to your lungs. It doesn't look good."

He removed his reading glasses and looked at me very seriously, almost like the vice principal staring me down when I got caught cutting class.

"There's a pretty nasty infection down there. If we don't get it under control, you'll probably lose part of your lung. What in hell were you doing—playing in a sewer?"

I wanted to choke the bastard. Instead, Dr. Rickles choked me the next day by sticking a long, hard tube deep into my lungs. He took tissue samples and sucked out whatever mucus he could find. I nearly died from that damn snaking tube. I had to raise my hand to indicate that I had enough like I was a loser in a wrestling match. When he yanked the damn thing out, I thought he was pulling some of my vocal cords with it. He kept telling me about a swarm of rare and contagious bacteria eating away at my bronchi, and that's why I was bleeding. The sonovabitch was trying to scare me.

It worked.

"I guess I'll have to stay in the hospital for a few days, Mom," I told her over the phone. *At least I'll have better food here,* I thought as I held up the lunch menu by the light. I checked-off the Salisbury steak, mashed potatoes, applesauce, and requested two brownies for dessert.

The next day the doctor came in and asked me what was wrong with my mother and why she wasn't in the psych ward. I shrugged my shoulders and acted stupidly. "I dunno. She's not that bad."

He said that he didn't understand a damn thing she said and that she should be on some strong neuroleptics, preferably anti-psychotics.

I didn't say anything. I just looked at the nurse's warm hands strapping the blood pressure cuff to my arm. She did it so gently, so lovingly that I didn't mind her groping me. I looked forward to wearing the blood pressure cuff each day, the thermometer stuck in my mouth, and having my forehead touched by her dainty fingers.

"Well, anyway, give it a few days, and you'll be as good as new," Dr. Rickles said.

Good as new, my ass. I heard that shit before. That's the seal of death. That means I'll be screwed-up for life, and I'll have a portable oxygen tank on wheels to push around into my old age. Okay, Doc. Put me on disability. Diagnose me like a pathetic loser, a human being who can't work, can't go to school, and has to live off the government for the rest of his life.

Sure enough, the doctor was a liar. My hospital stay wasn't just for a few days. It took three weeks to clean out the infection and to get me breathing okay again. The nurses hooked my arm to an IV, giving me a 24/7 stream of antibiotics into my veins, and changing the drip bag every few hours. I had to walk around the unit with an IV contraption on wheels by my side like it was a conjoined twin.

"Be careful," said the nurse. "Don't pull your tubes out."

"Don't worry," I said, "I won't do anything stupid."

So, there I was, a lonely and bored asthmatic. Most of the time, I hung out in the patient lounge, watching some lame game show on TV. Then when I thought my life was just about the lowest it could be, a pretty girl with bangs came into the patient lounge and also hooked up to an IV. With gorgeous red hair and pale milky skin, she sat right next to me on the sofa. Instantly, I felt a kinship. She was frail and vulnerable and had a pair of compromised lungs as well. What more could I ask? She was kind of sexy in a feeble way, but I didn't know if I was horny in general or if I liked her. All I knew was that I wanted to hump her brains out in the patient's lounge, right next to the Magnavox TV, across from the nurse's station full of chatty nurses and interns.

"Hi, my name is Harry," I said, feeling an immediate connection.

"Landie. Landie Willoughby."

We talked about things we hated in school and rock groups that we liked, flirted and laughed as the nurses periodically changed our IV bags and took whatever vital signs they needed.

There was something about our IV bags dripping at the same moment, like two ballroom dancers sharing a perfect rhythm. Both of us seemed to enjoy watching our bags dripping a clear liquid into our veins, knowing that we were slowly ridding ourselves of those microscopic infections that made our lives miserable.

For dinner, we had roast beef au jus with green beans almondine and mashed potatoes. I wanted to nibble on Landie instead of my dinner. But the roast beef wasn't that bad, and the string beans weren't as overcooked as my mother made them.

At night Landie rested her head on my lap. I was wearing a white-and-blue hospital gown commando. My lap slowly transformed into a colossal boner catching us by surprise, and indicating that my overall health was improving.

"You don't mind?" I asked politely.

Without saying a word, she rubbed my penis with the back of her head so discreetly that the nurses didn't suspect anything. They were too busy filling out their nightly paperwork and distributing medications in tiny white cups.

I felt pretty perky the next day. I got Doctor Rickles to release me on Friday if I promised to take all my medicine and to see a pulmonologist and allergist regularly.

I would agree to anything. I would obey my Mom, stop stealing, and even take my corny textbooks home from school. "Sure, Doc. No problem."

Landie Willoughby left a couple of days after I did. We exchanged phone numbers, and I promised to call her once I got out of the hospital. But she wasn't Sandy Finkle. Whatever we had turned out to be only a hospital fling. It felt romantic inside the hospital's antiseptic walls, but once I got my freedom, I started to think of her more as an asthmatic than a sex object. I know it sounds harsh, but I didn't want anything or anybody to remind me that I had chronic asthma. I didn't want to be associated with that torture chamber that everyone called a hospital.

12

My parents were not my parents in the parental sense. They didn't care about me and often seemed too preoccupied with themselves. They tried to convince me that I was like everyone else; that I could run a marathon, jump over tall buildings in a single bound, smoke a pack of cigarettes a day—anything that I wanted to do. They denied that I had a severe case of asthma, even in the face of my hospitalization. "Oh, you'll outgrow it," my Mom said. My father thought it was all in my head even though I coughed up blood and wheezed so much that I couldn't get off the damn stoop.

Sure, Mom, I'll outgrow it. Sure, Dad, it's all in my head. So what if the pulmonologist said that I had a pair of ninety-year-old lungs in a fifteen-year-old body. What does the pulmonologist know?

After I came home from the hospital, my father, of all things, brought a toy poodle puppy into my life. The allergist explicitly stated to my parents that I should not have any pets in the house, except for tropical fish.

"My customer had a litter of puppies," Dad said. "They were so cute that I couldn't say no."

He knew that I loved dogs and thought that I might forget he was a sonovabitch if he bestowed on me an adorable toy poodle.

The first day in the house, I could feel the dander crawling up my skin. Snot ran down my nose like an avalanche of green mucus. I could feel my bronchioles tightening up like twisted wires and my heart beating like a tom-tom. In a matter of minutes, I had become hooked on the puppy, regardless of how he affected my health.

The dog was my savior, my best friend, and my worst enemy all wrapped into one.

Of course, the doctor visits increased as well as the doses of allergy and asthma medications. They stepped up my allergy shots to once a week and told me again—*get rid of the dog!*

Nope. Not gonna do it. The dog stays no matter what. You

could put me in an iron lung or inside a great, big antiseptic bubble, but I'm never getting rid of the toy poodle!

As long as I had the dog, nothing else mattered. I loved that canine more than my parents and, perhaps, myself. I looked forward to being with the dog when I got home from school or after playing stickball with Bergman and Padidas. The dog sat on my tummy as we watched *The Three Stooges* reruns and crawled into the bed with me when I rooted for the Seventy-Sixers against the Celtics. I named him Richie after my favorite Phillies baseball player, Richie Allen, the power-hitting third baseman.

Richie had white curly fur, black-button eyes, and a stump-like wagging tail. He knew how much I suffered from asthma and tried to heal me with his wet sandpaper tongue all over my face. Richie could hear my wheezing, rattling lungs, and the gurgling congestion. He didn't like it one bit and attempted to bark it away.

Then after a few months of boy-dog bliss, my mother had to screw it all up again. She decided to paint the inside of the house without telling anyone. She made no mention to the painters that a dog was at home and liable to run away if a door was left open.

The day the painters came was the day Richie disappeared. I was at school and had no idea that he was running after cars and wandering down random streets in our neighborhood searching for me, howling in homeless dog agony. Of course, my mother, who was in the house all day, had no clue that Richie was missing. She was too busy having a conversation with herself and deciding if the cream-colored walls were too light for her living room furniture.

Once home from school, I freaked out on my mother. "Why didn't you close the damn door! Why didn't you tell the painters that we had a goddamn dog!" I yelled. I got so mad that I put my hands around her neck, and if she hadn't kicked me in the balls with her pointed high-heels, I would have been a murderer.

I left the house and rode my bike up and down the streets looking for Richie. I stapled hastily written flyers on the telephone poles, and, for two weeks, I looked under parked cars, scoured the alleyways and dumpsters for my missing pooch.

Wouldn't you know it, once I stopped looking and gave up all hope, someone called to say that Animal Control had picked up a dog that looked like Richie. I was so happy. I thought I was going to get my dog back despite everything.

Once inside Animal Control, however, we quickly learned that life sucked again. There was no reprieve to my mental suffering, only a shit-storm.

"Oh, sorry," the woman at the counter said while flashing her long fingernails. "We had a dog fitting that description, but we just put him to sleep just a few hours ago."

I reached a critical point in my life that I never thought would happen. It was almost as if the structure of my brain changed, and I could think better. A couple of weeks ago, I had nearly choked my mother, and could feel the anger in my body boil to the point where I wanted to hurt someone else. There was nothing for me to do but to stop and reconfigure.

The school counselor recently told me, "It's time to think in a way that doesn't hurt so much, Harry."

He told me that my anger isn't about my mother or father; it's about me and that I'm the only person who could stop it.

"Your anger isn't going to bring back Richie or solve your school problems or heal your mother's mental illness."

My rage wouldn't make my asthma go away, either, I thought.

I had to change.

I turned to my father at Animal Control that day and couldn't believe what came out of my mouth.

"Richie ran away for my own sake, Dad. He sacrificed himself because he knew that I was allergic to him, and he couldn't stand making me sick anymore. My life will work out. I'm sure of it. The universe wants me to be happy even though it hasn't appeared that way so far. The only way I will get out of this mess is if I change the way I look at things."

This time my father stuttered. "Wah-wah-well, you might be right, Harry. But what do you mean, the universe wants you to be happy?"

"I can't answer that, Dad. Just trust me on it."

Two weeks after Richie died, my asthma cleared up. Not perfect, but much better. It was hard for me to believe. I really did have the power to change.

13

By Thanksgiving, I had forgotten all about Richie. My asthma was so under control that I had stopped taking allergy shots. And my father had made it home for Thanksgiving. He invited all our relatives for dinner—Grandma, my uncles, my aunts, and my two cousins. It was the only time that I had a real family Thanksgiving, not the kind with just me and Mom eating fatty corned beef on rye from the Casino Deli. No, this was a real Thanksgiving with actual relatives, a carved turkey in the middle of the dining room table, surrounded by baked potatoes, pies, yams, cranberry sauce, buttered carrots and, of course, Grandma's stuffing with fried chicken livers.

There was Mom, the ultimate agitator, and ball-breaker. She was the crazy woman from Borneo who couldn't stop talking to herself if her life depended on it.

Dad was the asshole supreme. He was a self-centered egomaniac that most people viewed as a nice guy. But if you lived with him, you'd know that he was the horniest guy on earth and would sell his firstborn to get a good piece of tail.

Uncle Leo probably had the biggest shlong in Pennsylvania and was a chronic alcoholic. He liked to sleep at social gatherings with his hands in his pants, holding his precious crown jewels. Uncle Leo was oblivious to the people around him and most comfortable when he was drunk. He would much rather be sitting on a stool at a Pottsville pub telling a waitress a dirty joke than being home with his loyal and loving wife, Aunt Mary.

Uncle Sy, the most handsome man of the family, had pearly white teeth, jet-black hair, and used way too much cologne. He was more in love with himself than any of the beautiful goddess-like women he dated. He should have been a movie star instead of a guy hawking jewelry on Market Street in Center City.

Grandma Edna. She looked like Bette Davis with big bulging eyes and bright red hair, and was just as dramatic, if not more so. Grandma's crooked finger scared the hell out of anyone who's ever had constipation (I'll explain that later in graphic detail).

Aunt Mary was my favorite aunt, plump and affable. She adored Uncle Leo to a fault and got fat from Cheetos and bags of Wise Potato Chips while waiting for Uncle Leo to come home from a night of binge drinking. The fatter she got, the more loving and forgiving to Uncle Leo she became.

Aunt Marlene. The first and only time I would ever see her. She lived far away in a ritzy Boston suburb where snooty people looked down at those who lived in middle-class neighborhoods. We were paupers, crude, and unrefined in her eyes. "Too good for anyone living in Philly," my father often said.

Brent was Aunt Marlene's son. I wished I could have seen him more often. He liked sports, had bright red hair, and enjoyed being goofy like me. Although he was a Red Sox fan, he was a genuine kid with a kind disposition. He wasn't at all like his mother.

Lana, my sweet but unfortunate cousin, would die of cystic fibrosis in a couple of years. The little that I knew of her, I liked. It's usually the frail ones who are cursed with bad luck and leave this planet too early.

The family looked happy at the beginning but seemed to get progressively more distraught as the night wore on. My mother's constant babbling caused tension in the house. Grandma Edna kept telling her to shut up, "You don't have to talk so much, Lil. Just sit down and listen for a while."

Dad took his mind off my mother by filming everyone with

his 8mm Kodak movie camera. It was the first big thing he purchased once he got home from the Army. It was his way of doing something with his hands besides feeling up women.

Mom knew that people were trying their best to avoid her, which infuriated her even more. She eyed the people in the room and went over to each person and said at least one random thing to get their goat. It was very strategic, and for the most part, it worked. She called my Grandma Edna an old witch; told Aunt Mary to shave her legs; hinted that Aunt Marlene should have her tubes tied, and told Uncle Sy that he was a closet homosexual. When it came to my father, she called him several things—a fat slob and a baldheaded sonovabitch to name just a few. Dad's head turned bright red like a bulb blinking on a Christmas tree.

14

I tried not to look at Cousin Lana, who was coughing up cystic fibrosis plugs the size of tennis balls, and spitting them into the trash. While Cousin Lana was coughing up one particularly gruesome plug, my mother opened the window of her second-floor bedroom. She announced to everyone downstairs that she was going to jump two stories to the concrete walkway below because no one was willing to talk to her.

"Everyone thinks I'm a bad person," she moaned.

I watched Uncle Sy scramble upstairs in his shiny black leather shoes, nearly tripping over my Converse on the bottom step. Everyone got quiet like something dramatic was about to happen. My father kept rolling the camera, making believe that whatever happens would be worthy of a good family memory.

We listened to the cries and horrible sobbing by my mother. Then the window slammed, a lamp broke, a piercing cry, and stomping footsteps. My mother raced downstairs in her bare feet and threw herself on the sofa in tears.

She couldn't stop bawling. Dad didn't know what to do, so he kept shooting, of course. He probably would have won an

Academy Award for the best documentary in the category of "Family Drama" if my father remembered to load film in the camera.

Grandma rolled her bulging eyes and made a crazy sign with her crooked finger.

Aunt Mary was still sitting on my Uncle Leo's lap, rubbing his bald head like Aladdin's lamp while he had his hand in his pants, holding his magic wand.

My cousins watched reruns of the *Soupy Sales Show* with White Fang's big paw reaching out while Aunt Marlene told them to ignore my mother as if she were a gruesome monster herself. It was common knowledge that Aunt Marlene wanted my mother hospitalized so she wouldn't have to visit her in Philly anymore.

I smiled through all the tension and drama. Despite what was happening, it was the best Thanksgiving I ever had. It was my family, and they were all beautiful in a very dysfunctional way.

15

Soon, a couple of chunky men in windbreakers from the hospital carrying clipboards and a duffle bag entered the house. Dad put down his camera for a second and explained what happened upstairs. Uncle Sy said that my mother needed immediate help. "She's out of control," he said, still smelling of expensive cologne with his hair perfectly in place. Grandma added, "It would be best for her if she went into a place where she got her head straightened out."

Mom vehemently refused to go with the two men. She bolted for the door. Fast on his feet, Uncle Sy blocked her escape. The biggest man showed my mother a straitjacket and explained that it wasn't an option he wanted to take, "I'd do it if it meant keeping you safe, ma'am." The other burly man, who identified himself as a physician's assistant, injected her with a sedative in the behind. Eventually, my mother calmed down enough for the two men to reason with her. Brainwashed and docile, she left the house quietly, head down with hopelessness, and not one goodbye as she walked out the door.

Only tears.

"Crocodile tears," Grandma said.

"Thank God there was no scene," Dad told Grandma, finally realizing that there was no film in the camera.

Aunt Marlene had a strange *I-told-you-so* grin on her face and said, "Everything works out for the best."

My cousins were now watching Bing Crosby's *White Christmas*, barely awake, and stretched out on the floor. Lana finished her treatment and was breathing just fine.

Uncle Leo was still holding his nuts, and Aunt Mary was cleaning out his dirty ears with the end of one of her fake fingernails.

Grandma Edna turned to me and lit up with the biggest smile, "You're going to live with me now, Harry. Isn't that wonderful?"

I watched as Mom got into the red and white van with the two big crisis workers. I saw Bergman and Padidas on the stoop talking to each other, probably making jokes about how crazy my Mom was and wondering if I was a wacko, too. Even Sandy, the girl I loved, with the long auburn hair down to her butt, was outside on the steps watching with interest. I hoped that she didn't think I was crazy, also.

I took two puffs of my emergency inhaler even though I wasn't feeling asthmatic.

16

I eventually enjoyed living with Grandma. She was much more stable than my parents, and she was relatively fun to be around. Every Saturday afternoon, we went to Corbin Hall for bingo. We each bought four bingo cards. "It's better that way," Grandma said. "Increases our chances of winning."

I was the only person who had real teeth at Corbin Hall. My nose was itchy from all the hairspray. There was a faint smell of urine that increased with time. I know my Grandma had a leaky bladder, but I didn't realize that most of the other elderly had it worse. Grandma said that the guy with the bifocals was probably wearing extra-absorbency adult diapers because of his bulky backside. She pointed to a chubby lady named Gladys, who had the worst case of psoriasis, not to mention halitosis. I had to focus really hard on my four bingo cards to keep from throwing up.

A senior named Artie with thick bifocals and a seersucker sports jacket was barely able to stand straight at the podium. He called out the letters and the numbers while every so often clearing his throat and blowing his nose into a hanky. The balls popped up from his spinning machine. Grandma chewed on a couple of Chiclets while she looked down from her glasses and placed the red plastic circles on the numbers. She was in a different world when she played bingo, forgetting about her lousy heart and her hammertoes.

A couple of times, I came close. I just needed a B-5 and an I-20. Grandma won a couple of games and cashed in her coupons for a little striped change purse much like the other five or six she had in her bedroom dresser. It was probably a good thing I didn't win because there were only prizes for seniors like magnifying glasses and Betty Boop trinkets I couldn't use anyway.

Grandma taught me what it meant to be a senior citizen. I adapted to her early bedtime without resistance. I didn't mind watching *The Lawrence Welk Show* and even the corny Lennon Sisters singing a cappella. I didn't barf when Grandma ate borscht with sour cream or soaked her gnarly feet with Epsom salts in a large cat-litter tray. I didn't mind when she walked out of the shower holding her sagging boobs in her hands or cutting farts that smelled like rotten eggs.

If you ever met Grandma Edna, you'd notice several things about her: her hair was bright, henna red and puffed up with hairspray. Her green eyes bulged out of her eye sockets, something fierce. And her forefinger on her right hand was severely bent like Captain Hook, crooked from the many years of rheumatoid arthritis.

It was that forefinger that scared me the most as a kid. It doesn't bother me now, but when I was younger, I had an experience with that damn arthritic finger that I'd soon like to forget.

When I was ten, I was sitting on the couch, watching Grandma's favorite program, *The Lawrence Welk Show*. Grandma was in her puffy red chair with a cup of Lipton tea and saltine crackers on a small folding table.

"Excuse me, Grandma, I have to go to the bathroom."

She didn't hear me. She was fixated on Lawrence Welk, who probably made her horny, and didn't notice anything except those stupid bubbles bouncing off the screen. I didn't blame her for not hearing me leave the room, going to the bathroom was a rather mundane thing, but on that day in the middle of August, it turned out to be quite an ordeal.

The problem was that I couldn't move my bowels. I could pee all right, but my poop stuck in Never Land. No matter how much I willed that damn turd to come out—that sonovabitch wouldn't budge. So, I spent most of *The Lawrence Welk Show* in the bathroom squeezing and straining while Grandma sipped her pekoe tea with lemon, noshed on saltines, and hummed along to some goofy Lawrence Welk tune.

The previous day, my Grandma complained that I never eat enough fiber and that all I ever eat is bread and meat. I told her that I didn't like peas or lettuce or any of the other vegetables she recommended. Just give me a thick corned beef sandwich and a Tastykake apple pie, and I'd be happy. She even offered me some prunes, but unfortunately, I refused. I had no idea that I would ever get constipated and didn't understand the concept of *being regular*.

"Is everything all right in there?" Grandma shouted from the living room when she realized that she hadn't seen me in a while. "You've been in there for an hour."

"Not so good, Grandma," I moaned while straining.

"What's the problem, honey?"
"It won't come out!"
"What won't come out?"
"My turd. The damn thing is stuck!"
"Push harder!" she cried.
"I'm trying!"

She jumped from her recliner once the Geritol commercial was over, opening the door of the bathroom, and swooping in on me like Catwoman. Once she saw my skinny white butt sitting on her beige toilet seat in constipation misery, she sprang into action.

"Let me fix it," she said as she wielded her crooked finger in the air like it was a magic saber that could cure all my anal ills.

"No!" I screamed. "Not the finger!"

"Don't worry; you won't feel a thing. I'll dig the damn thing out before you could whistle Dixie."

I had no idea what she meant by *whistling Dixie*, but before I could ask, Grandma lunged at me.

I barely eluded her and ran out of the bathroom with my shorts and underwear to my ankles. I barely eluded her grasp, and hopped into the living room, squeezing my sphincters in vice-like fashion.

We both stopped in our tracks when there was a knock on the front door. *Oh, good*, I thought. *Somebody's going to save me from the finger.*

"Come in!" Grandma yelled. "We're in here!"

It was my father in his work boots and khakis. Grandma must have called him while I was wedged behind the breakfront for a good half-hour. I had no clue he was in town.

"Where is he?" my father asked impatiently.

"He's behind the good china."

Oh, shit, I thought. *Now both Grandma and Dad were after me.*

"Don't worry," Dad said in a reassuring voice. "Grandma won't hurt you. She only wants you to feel better."

Dad told me to bend over as Grandma tried to insert a suppository that looked like a bullet from Roy Rogers' revolver.

"Ah, shit. It won't go in," Grandma said in frustration. "I can't get past the turd. It's like a brick."

Holy Christ! I thought to myself, imagining my Granny's crooked finger stuck up my asshole for all eternity.

"Let's take him to the hospital," Dad finally said in frustration. "We're wasting our time. Up the creek without a paddle."

A sense of hope shone brightly through the window. Maybe the hospital had a particular instrument with soft fingers to dislodge the damn thing. It was like going to a plumber to fix a bathroom sink, not a Grandma with a crooked finger. The only thing she knew how to fix was a pot roast in a pressure cooker and, even then, she put in the carrots and potatoes too early.

As I rode in the backseat of my father's truck, I kept staring at Grandma's finger as if it were a separate entity about to come alive. I figured if I knew where it was, the finger wouldn't make any surprise attacks.

At the hospital, I felt much safer. People were considerate and didn't laugh at me when I told them that a turd was stuck in my butt. The nurses placed me in a white room with bright lights. I remember the nurse told me that it would be over in a few seconds and not to worry. "Turn over on your side," she said in a sweet and reassuring voice. She held my hand as a cold, sharp instrument pinched my butt. The doctor said, "Just rest for a few minutes until it takes effect." I felt groggy and blurted out several incomprehensible sentences. I think I asked the doctor if Grandma's crooked finger was still up my ass. He laughed. "Oh, no, son. I wouldn't let that happen to you."

The nurse thoughtfully covered my butt cheeks with a white bed sheet so I wouldn't catch a cold. I closed my eyes and drifted off.

I didn't know the name of the contraption that entered my anus, but I didn't want to ask. Whatever it was, I was sure that it would be a whole lot better than Grandma's crooked forefinger. I was confident that my ass was in safe hands with the attending doctor and the kind nurse, optimistic that my agony would soon be over, and my tuchus could finally be a normal butt again. Several hours later, I woke in my own bed. My anus was a little sore, but it could have been a lot worse.

17

I had no trouble with constipation after that. I could ride a bike, play stickball, and harass my teachers without the least bit of anal discomfort. I could also visit my crazy Grandpa and sit on one of those hard plastic chairs in the cafeteria and watch him roll up a napkin into an arrowhead and drill it into his dried-up nostril like he was digging for oil.

At least once a week, Grandma and I got on the 66 Bus to visit Grandpa Izzy, who lived in a room at the Boulevard Falls Nursing Home. Even though he was in the mid-eighties, Grandpa Izzy still had a head like a watermelon but probably a brain the size of a pea. He had severe dementia; Alzheimer's, it was called, but Grandma sometimes referred to it as "hardening of the arteries," which just confused me. Whatever it was, it was only getting worse. Every time we saw him, it was more difficult for him to recognize us, and he kept asking for the same favor.

"Kiddidlehopper, will you go to the corner store and get me a pack of those Conestoga stogies that I like?"

"Grandpa," I said. "They don't allow people to smoke here."

When I refused, he called me a "lazy little fucker." Grandma said not to mind Grandpa because he had hardening of the arteries. "He always forgets so it doesn't matter what you tell him," Grandma said. "Just smile and say no."

We all sat in the lounge area that smelled like someone pooped on the floor. We watched a TV with rabbit ears that had terrible reception no matter how many ways you positioned the antenna. I think the *Beverly Hillbillies* was on, but it could have been *Green Acres* or *Petticoat Junction*.

"Kiddidlehopper!!" he yelled, referring to me. "Get me one of those stogies at the corner store, will yah?! Here's a dollar," taking a rolled-up piece of paper out of his pocket and handing it to me.

I ignored him, like Grandma had said. She was busy knitting a green and white afghan to keep his veiny legs warm while he was sitting in the lounge area in just a hospital robe. When he sat with his legs spread, you could see his loose-fitting underwear and part of his privates.

"Get me the damn stogie!" he shouted and rattled his walker with the tennis balls stuck to its metal legs.

"Now, now, Mr. Tobin," said his nursing attendant. "You know your grandson isn't allowed to purchase stogies. He's way too young. And besides, you're not allowed to smoke in the hospital."

"Damn, sonuvabitch," Grandpa muttered. "What the hell is he good for!"

I turned to Grandma and smiled. "How about if we buy him a pack of candy cigarettes so he would have something to put in his mouth?"

"He'll know the difference," Grandma said. "He has Alzheimer's, but he's not stupid."

Grandpa Izzy seemed to know everyone on television. No matter who it was, he was his friend, a family member, or a former customer when he was in the junk business. Whether it was *The Mod Squad* or *The Partridge Family*, he could tell you how he met them and details about their lives.

"Humphrey Bogart used to be my drinking buddy when he lived in Mahanoy City."

"Katharine Hepburn was my dancing partner at the Maroon Club on Manatunga Street."

He once dated Ginger Rogers. He knew her father from when he was hawking produce off a truck in Minersville.

He called Grandma Lucille Ball because of her bright red hair. He kept asking her where Desi was because he wanted to screw her brains out before he came home from the club.

But for me, I was always the "kiddidlehopper," whatever that meant. And if I didn't get Grandpa a stogie, I was a "lazy little fucker."

18

After Grandpa Izzy died in his sleep, naked and spread-eagled, we cremated him and put his urn on the curio with a box of his favorite stogies right next to it. I would always pass the urn and say hello to Grandpa, ask him if he was okay and if he wanted me to go to the corner store to get him a pint of Yuengling or a box of his favorite cigars. Once in a while, I swore he called me a "lazy little fucker."

We had more time to visit my mother in the hospital after Grandpa died, which wasn't a lot different from seeing Grandpa Izzy in the nursing home, except that a mental institution didn't smell like poop. Its fragrance was more like bleach, and dirty socks and the people weren't half dead like a nursing home but acted bizarrely as people do on Halloween.

I barely recognized Mom. She wore a flimsy cotton hospital gown and spoke to us in garbled whispers. Her lips were dry and cracked, and her tongue seemed to snake out of her mouth uncontrollably. Her head was so stiff that she couldn't swivel it to the left or right. She stared at us with strings of saliva dripping from her mouth that reminded me of a Harpo Marx harp. Grandma kept handing her a tissue to catch the drool. She took it and held it at the wrong spot while the spittle fell to the right of the target.

The psychiatrist met with us privately. He explained that Mom was getting a special treatment where electrodes were attached to her head, and a series of jolts of electricity stimulated the cerebral cortex. "This will hopefully snap her out of whatever depression she's in," the doctor said confidently. He didn't see me roll my eyes, but I wanted to know how getting zapped with electricity would make anyone less crazy. It's like sticking your fingers into an electrical outlet and expecting to become another Einstein.

After about ten electricity treatments, it was hard to imagine her ever getting better. She kept fading away like an elusive dream; no matter how hard you tried to recall who she once was, you couldn't. I tried to picture what she looked like before it all this happened. I vaguely remember her wearing bright cherry lipstick, and her hair was always nicely done even though she was crazy. She used to laugh a lot, mainly to herself, and the sound of her voice was clear. Yes, she talked to herself too much back then and wanted to jump out of a window a couple of times, but she was alive. In the hospital, she seemed like a zombie in slow motion.

We sat with her in the family lounge of the hospital and watched *Dragnet* reruns on a fuzzy TV screen. She sat like a mound of clay, not moving from her spot at the end of the sofa, staring blankly at the TV screen as if it were going to tell her something profound.

"Mom? Mom? Are you okay?" I kept asking, but she never responded in the way I expected. We tried to ignore the strings of drool from her lips. But it kept falling off her mouth and dripping on her hospital gown. It would drive us crazy, but we smiled like Grandma said and just ignored it.

Sitting there with my mother, I realized something. Even if she could come back to earth, I didn't want to change anything. I didn't want to go back to the way it was when she was my crazy mother throwing empty Coke bottles at my friends and embarrassing me in front of Sandy. I didn't want to deal with all those miserable ups and downs that she had that drove me nuts. Grandma was a little eccentric and had a wickedly crooked finger, but she was stable. Right now, stable was the best I could hope.

19

Once we came home from the hospital, Grandma opened the top drawer of the curio cabinet and took out a deck of cards she kept in an old, yellowing Ziploc plastic bag. She shuffled the deck with her bony arthritic fingers, flipping and fanning them with her thumbs like a casino dealer.

She was good at cards, maybe could have been a card shark in a different lifetime, dealing two and sometimes three cards at a time without even counting out loud. She didn't go easy on me, but played to win like a real hustler, all the while reminding me of the rules which I tended to forget.

I looked at her in awe as she racked up the points—her red hair seemed to glow brighter with each hand that she won. Her bugged-out eyes seemed to jump out of its sockets with each victory.

She never grew tired of playing cards, even when she was short of breath or her heart pounded feverishly in her chest. She just put a nitroglycerin tablet under her tongue, took a little sip of ginger ale to ease the harsh taste of the pill, and kept dealing.

We eventually got hungry after four or five games of Rummy and Casino, and she got out the ceramic bowls from the kitchen cabinet. Like a dog sensing food, I knew what the clanking of the bowls meant.

"Do you want to help me make some tuna fish?" she'd ask, already knowing the answer.

It was Grandma Edna's magical food, something that I thought she invented for the longest time. Her tuna salad was like a horse tranquilizer; it numbed me out, made me forget all the rotten times in my life, and made me think only about pleasant things. It transported me to a state of euphoria, where the world was friendly and sunny like a Disney cartoon.

Grandma cranked her old-fashioned can opener. Its sound became an earworm, much like *Wooly Bully,* that also kept playing in my head. She boiled two large eggs and peeled one small baby onion. Her bulging eyes filled with buckets of tears, but it didn't stop her. She put the tuna into the mixing bowl with some diced onions and celery. She passed me a top-handle knife, and I chopped with both hands as if I did it for a living. Every so often, Grandma added a large glob of mayonnaise to make the tuna extra creamy.

"Watch your fingers," she said and pointed her crooked forefinger at me to drive home the point.

She added the two hard-boiled eggs, and I chopped some more. An extra dollop of mayonnaise for good measure, and then I'd whip the tuna. The four slices of Wonder Bread popped out of the toaster just brown enough.

As we ate our toasted tuna sandwiches and drank our Cokes from the bottle, Grandma said that she knew that she loved me ever since I was a baby. She said that I was so cute and chubby that she couldn't keep her hands off my girthy body. She thought it was a shame that I didn't have a mother who was able to love me and a father who'd make raising a son a priority. After the first bite of her second sandwich, Grandma's heart hurt again. "Angina," she called it and muttered *sonovabitch* under her breath with each sharp pain that she felt. She held onto the enamel sink in the kitchen and called for me to get the nitroglycerin tablets in the medicine cabinet. She put a pill under her tongue, and I wiped the sweat from her brow with a damp cloth. She sat down for a few minutes to catch her breath and then continued to eat her sandwich.

I worried that Grandma would die and leave me alone. I took a couple of puffs from my inhaler to ease the tightness in my chest. Grandma said that she needed to schedule an appointment with Dr. Links, my allergist, since I seemed to be using the inhaler more frequently. While she worried about my lungs, I worried about her bad heart. Grandma had to live a few more years until I finished school. I know that sounded selfish, but she was my anchor; without her, I'd surely drown.

20

Dr. Links looked like a young Charlton Heston, tan and handsome, and ready to ride a Roman chariot. Instead of a chariot, however, he had a stationary bike in his office that he probably used while his patients were waiting impatiently in the numbered rooms, wondering where the hell he was. Dr. Links was born with a silver spoon in his mouth, probably in some swanky

Main Line suburb with filthy rich parents, and expected everyone to be as healthy and as smart as he was. If you didn't meet his expectations or respect his vast knowledge of the human body, you better look out. He would view you with pity and say something condescending that would most likely make you feel like a pile of shit.

He made me nervous when he gave me the dreaded breathing test. He'd clip my nose with a plastic clothespin and tell me to blow into the tube as hard and as long as I could. So, to please him, I would inhale as deeply as possible, hold it in, and blast it out with all my might. I wanted Dr. Links to be proud of me, impressed by the numbers on the spirometer.

"You could do better, Harry," he said. "You're not trying your best."

"But I feel dizzy."

"That's normal. Don't worry, just blow."

He pointed to the score that he circled in red ink, "Not bad. Last month you were much better, though."

I wanted to say, "What the hell do you want from me? If I could blow any harder, I would. If I blow too damn hard, a couple of my blood vessels might pop and then you'd send me back into the hospital with a brain aneurysm."

Instead, I just nodded in deference to the deity in the white robe, to Charlton Heston, who rode the Roman chariot.

After several failed attempts, Dr. Links finally gave up. He sent in one of his nurses to do allergy testing. Thank God he left, probably on the phone with his wife planning some European vacation while doing the Tour de France on his stationary bike.

"Please, remove your shirt and lay face down on the table," the nurse said sweetly.

I could get horny anywhere. I fantasized about the nurse jumping naked on my back and humping me with reckless abandon. I didn't care if she was the nurse for the world's most arrogant allergist. Her gentle hands made little love imprints all over my back that must have triggered my sexual nerve endings. Slowly she stuck one pin in, then another, and then circled and labeled each pinprick with a ballpoint pen. "That's for dog allergies, grass, mold," and on and on until there was no skin on my back left to stick.

"I feel like a human pincushion," I said, "but I'm not complaining."

"Everyone says that," she said and, after the last pinprick, told me to rest on the table for a while, and she'd be back in about twenty minutes. There was nothing to look at besides the rolled out white paper beneath me on the examination table. I kept waiting to hear her delicate footsteps approach the door. It was like waiting for Santa to come down the chimney and bring me some presents, except that she had a much better figure.

Once she returned, she gently touched the swells on my back, wrote something down on a clipboard, and scrubbed the ink markings off my skin. I put my shirt back on, and the nurse said, "The doctor will return in a few minutes with the results." A few minutes turned into an hour, of course. I leafed through a couple of old *Field and Stream* magazines to see how annoying fishing was. I tried on some of the doctor's medical gloves and gave myself a complete exam. I checked my heart with the stethoscope, still beating. I grabbed a few tissues and blew my nose and cleaned the wax from my ears with a Q-tip, surprised that there was so much waxy buildup.

The doctor came in without knocking as I was sticking two tongue depressors up my nostrils. His reading glasses hung over his nose as he looked me up and down. He scanned the chart. "Looks pretty bad," he said. "You are allergic to just about everything. The list includes wheat, milk, eggs, dogs, cats, nuts, mold, grass, trees, and about forty other things that aren't as common."

There was a long, pregnant pause as I could hear the doctor's heavy breathing, worse than mine. Looking up, I could see the inside of his nostrils and a few long gray nose hairs that seemed to be waving at me.

"I'm going to put you on several different medications to try and stabilize your wheezing, coughing, and shortness of breath. I'm also getting you back on allergy injections as soon as possible."

I didn't want to go on allergy shots again. I'd have to go to Dr. Links' office every week and watch him collect everybody's money and get stinkin' rich off of us poor, wheezy bastards.

"Why do the shots leave bruises and welts on your arms the size of baseballs?" I asked.

"You have a minor reaction. Put some ice on it."

I always agreed with the doctors. I thought that's what you were supposed to do, so I never questioned anything that they said. But this time I had more gonads than usual.

"Sorry, Doc. I'm not getting allergy shots again. My asthma's not that bad since I moved in with my Grandma and lost my poodle."

He looked offended. He sucked his teeth, rolled his eyes, and appeared as though he wanted to smash his clipboard over my head. He reminded me what a great doctor he was, and pointed to all the degrees hanging on the walls and the recordings of his multiple TV appearances. "How dare you refuse," he said. "I've been in practice since before you were born, Harry."

He told me that I was making a serious mistake, thinking that my asthma was under control as he removed his glasses from his nose and put it into his shirt pocket. He clumsily tore off a few prescriptions from his pad and told me that I could leave as soon as I buttoned my shirt and zipped up my pants.

Two months later, Dr. Links died from a coronary. I'm not sure where he died, but I wouldn't be surprised if it wasn't on his stationary bike. My belief about doctors was confirmed. They were not Gods.

21

I would reluctantly leave Grandma to stay with my aunt and uncle in Pottsville for the summer. Grandma assured me that she would be fine and would take care of herself in my absence. She'd go to the bingo hall with her friends who had bladder control problems. Grandma would chop the tuna by herself. If she needed milk or corned beef, she'd ask her neighbor to drive her to the deli. If she ran out of heart pills, she'd call the pharmacy and have them delivered. If she had a medical emergency, she knew the numbers to the hospital and the ambulance service.

"Don't worry," she said. "I'll be fine."

I had gone to Pottsville every summer for the last ten years. I worked with Uncle Leo during the day in his produce warehouse. I bagged potatoes and onions, helped load trucks, and stacked watermelons like pyramids on the warehouse floor. When things got slow, I hung out in Uncle Leo's stuffy office that smelled like cheap liquor and rotten onions. I sat on the stool in his office and listened to old Johnny Cash songs on his clock radio. I knew I wasn't in Philly with Grandma because we never listened to Tammy Wynette or Buck Owens. We didn't like that crap. However, in Pottsville, the music fits the mood of a small town. Pottsville was a place where people mined coal, worked long hours, got their boots dirty, and didn't care about coordinating their clothing or leaving a fart in a crowded room. As long as the barroom was open, they were happy.

Dad worked for my Uncle Leo at the beginning of the summer as a favor when my uncle was shorthanded. Dad often yelled at my uncle for drinking all the time and for carousing with tramps at the Falcon Club. One day a big fight ensued when Uncle Leo borrowed my father's new Chrysler New Yorker without asking and put a nice dent in his fender. Stenson, my uncle's drunken sidekick and a couple of other warehouse workers, restrained my father from killing Uncle Leo.

After about an hour of nasty insults and threats, the two brothers sat on the dirty warehouse floor crying. "I'm going to stop drinking," my uncle promised. "It's not doing me any good."

"I'm sorry I called you a drunken fuckface, Leo," my father apologized. "I should have known you couldn't help it."

It was all a bunch of bull. My uncle and father were both assholes who would never change. Uncle Leo had made promises before and never stopped drinking. He was probably an alcoholic in his crib. He drank six-packs when he was a toddler and progressed to whiskey by the time he reached thirteen. My father didn't believe my uncle would give up the bottle, either. "You can't change a zebra's stripes."

I found it ironic that my father always bagged on my uncle, especially about women. Dad cheated on my mother as long as I could remember, and he visited whorehouses and massage parlors every chance he got. From what I heard, he always selected women with big breasts and a generous rump. He justified his promiscuity because my mother was mentally ill and felt that he deserved some happiness. He wanted everyone's sympathy for marrying an insane woman. I didn't want to judge him, though. I was far from being an angel myself. All I knew was that in my heart, I didn't like that my Dad was with other women. It felt like he was cheating on me.

22

I watched Uncle Leo take one swig of whiskey after another. He made painful grimaces after each gulp, but it didn't stop him. There was always a new bottle, a new batch of alcohol to consume. He hid his whiskey in an empty Coke bottle, making believe that it was soda instead of booze as if people didn't know the difference. He smoked several packs of Camel cigarettes each day as he drank and chainsmoked into oblivion while he blew smoke rings up to the yellowing ceiling tiles. Merle Haggard always seemed to sing about some tramp that broke his heart on the clock radio as the office filled with smoke and the gross smell of rotten onions.

I didn't feel sorry for Uncle Leo. He was happy in his alcoholic misery. It was the only life he knew, and he resigned himself to that lifestyle to the day he died. I'm sure he believed that he couldn't change; he was too weak and too far gone to do anything different. He'd often cough or spit up blood, say his chest and back hurt, but he'd always return to the bottle like it was a woman that he could never let go. It was my thought that he believed that alcohol was healing him from life's pain and miseries and that it was the only medicine that he knew that worked.

When he ran out of whiskey, he got shaky and sweaty like one of his overripe tomatoes about to implode. It got so bad, that one day, I swore he was having an epileptic seizure. He shook so much that he couldn't talk to his customers over the phone or keep his pen straight enough to write down the produce orders. He smoked more and faster when he got the jitters. He drank tons of Coke, too, but that didn't work, either. Nothing replaced the bottle.

"I'll be right back," he said as a gallon of sweat poured down his brow. Without looking at me, he bolted for the door, leaving his burning cigarette in the ashtray, his pants slipping below his waist, and a roll of twenties tied by a rubber band still sitting on his desk next to the phone.

"Don't answer the phone, Harry. Let it ring," he mumbled on his way out.

I sat there as the phone kept ringing. I watched the cigarette burn down to ashes. "A Boy Named Sue" played on the radio. The linoleum floor in his office buckled and creaked when I walked back and forth. Invoices were all scattered about his desk with a capless ballpoint pen making an expanding ink stain on one of them. It smelled like one of Uncle Leo's big farts in the office, but it was just a five-pound bag of rotten potatoes in the corner with a bunch of happy flies circling it.

Sometimes I felt like Alfred E. Neuman with big jug ears, a stupid haircut, and a wide grin with a missing front tooth. I sat in the office like a complete dope waiting for Uncle Leo to return, knowing full well that his butt was glued to some barstool losing all track of time, inebriated beyond belief. If I knew my uncle, he probably gave one of those skanky waitresses a *titty-twister* and a friendly pinch on the butt.

At lunchtime, my uncle usually sent me around the corner to a sub shop, located next to a gas station that had a monkey inside a cage in the front window. I wondered why the guy at the gas station had a monkey for a pet. And wasn't it a shame that the monkey was trapped there. I often looked at it from across the street, too scared to go any closer, afraid of getting bit or scratched.

I wanted to peel off a twenty from Uncle Leo's money-bundle lying on the table. I was hungry for an Italian sub with extra sweet onions and provolone, a big bag of chips and a 32-ounce bottle of cherry Coke. Eating something tasty would have made me not feel so much like Alfred E. Newman.

My uncle never came back that day and didn't even call me to say that he was running late or just to see if I was okay. Aunt Mary picked me up about 2:30, and we had an early dinner. She made the best pot roast that I ever tasted. Her mashed potatoes were thick and creamy. The corn on the cob was splattered full of butter and salt. I had a big piece of German chocolate cake for dessert that Aunt Mary bought at the Acme supermarket earlier that day.

After dinner, we turned off the living room lights and watched an old movie called *The Quiet Man*, a John Wayne flick, filmed in Ireland with an actress named Maureen O'Hara. I thought it had a happy ending, the couple worked out their differences, but my aunt didn't think so. She kept crying.

I fell asleep on the couch about midnight, but I could feel my chest tighten when Uncle Leo stumbled into the house drunk, slamming the screen door behind him at 2:30 in the morning. My aunt cried, and all hell broke loose.

23

Uncle Leo wasn't all that bad. He loved me, and often took me to the bars and proudly showed me off to all his drinking buddies.

"Your nephew is good looking," his friends would say. "What happened to you, Leo?"

My uncle was a good sport, though, and didn't get mad at all the bald or ugly jokes.

One day Uncle Leo took me to his favorite bar, Dundees,

and I sat next to him on a barstool. Uncle Leo ordered me a Coke with ice and walked to a table to talk to some of his customers. I sat alone, staring at the pigs' knuckles floating in a glass jar. I wondered why people ate them; they looked so nasty like they would mess up your teeth when you chewed them. I wondered about a lot of things while I sat on the barstool in a dumpy bar.

"I'll have another Yuengling," Uncle Leo said to the bartender named Joanie. It was the only beer that Uncle Leo drank beside his favorite whiskey, Jack Daniel's. He let me take a swig of beer once, but I didn't care for the taste. The truth was, I didn't want to become an alcoholic like Uncle Leo.

Two dumpy barflies were giggling across from me. One, by the name of Peg, had a bouffant hairstyle, heavy on the makeup. The other, named Mary, was extremely skinny, with bright orange lipstick. They drank fruity mixed drinks with little umbrella straws. They didn't care what was playing on TV. All they wanted to do, it seemed, was spread gossip.

"Did you hear the latest on Miltie?" Peg asked her girlfriend.

"Miltie?"

"You know, the bald guy with the produce store on the highway."

"Oh, yeah, nice guy," said Mary.

"Lester Maroni is his boyfriend now. That's the guy who works for Pop Martin at the infirmary," Peg said while reaching for a handful of stale pretzels.

I looked up from my glass full of Coke, past the jar of pigs knuckles, at the two yapping women. Miltie was my father. He was the only Miltie in town who had a produce store on the highway. I nursed the Coke and kept my ears peeled.

"I hear he swings from both sides," Peg said. "But it's no secret that he likes dick better than pussy."

Dick better than pussy, I silently repeated to myself. I thought it over for a while. How could my old man feel that way toward men? I knew he wasn't having sex with my mother. She was in the hospital. I thought he had a girlfriend in Tamaqua; at least that's what Uncle Leo told me. He never told me that my Dad liked men, that's for sure. Why was it a big secret? Or was I the only person who didn't know?

"He's a cute one, too," Mary said. "How come all the good looking guys are queer?"

At least they thought that my Dad was cute.

"I don't know, Mary. I don't think I could go for a man who swings both ways. I don't want to be kissing a guy with penis breath."

I gulped down the rest of my Coke. The two women didn't know that I was Miltie's son. Even if they had, I'm sure it wouldn't have prevented them from gossiping about him.

"Joanie, I'll have another," Uncle Leo shouted. "And a Coke for my nephew, Harry."

"Handsome kid with good hair, too," said Joanie. "Sure doesn't take after you, Leo."

Joanie poured a couple of drinks and took three bucks from the bar. She filled the bowl with more stale pretzels and wiped the table with a grimy rag. Uncle Leo talked about the price of cabbage and how the farmers had a bad crop of red potatoes this year because of the drought.

I stared at the big-screen TV for a while. There was a Phillies game on. I thought about the time I went to Connie Mack Stadium with my father when I was a kid. We saw the Cubs with Ernie Banks playing shortstop. Banks hit a homer clear over the Coca-Cola sign in left field that landed on Lehigh Avenue. As the ball sailed over our heads, I remembered my Dad losing his hotdog, spilling the yellow mustard down the front of his white t-shirt. "The Phillies stink," he said, trying to wipe the stain out with a damp napkin. "They're not going to win squat if they play like this."

I thought I knew my Dad. He was Miltie, an asshole to Mom and me, but to everyone else, a friendly produce guy who craved women with big breasts; the size of Crenshaw Melons my uncle once told me. Now I hear that he goes down on men.

I thought about the time he lifted me high above the crowd to see the Mummer's Parade. I wasn't interested in polka music or the string bands, but I loved the fact that he was strong enough to lift me high above the crowd. I admired how he tossed hundred-pound sacks of potatoes on his shoulder and the way he stacked produce in a cooler without wasting space.

I almost choked on the stale pretzels that I mindlessly stuffed in my mouth. *That imposter*, I thought. Making believe that he liked women when in reality, he couldn't wait to be with a man.

The two bar hens stopped yakking, finally. They moved to the dance floor with two grimy yokels with muddy work boots and old flannel shirts. One guy was grinding Peg from behind while another was doing a slow dance with Mary to an Elvis tune.

Uncle Leo was missing all this. He was loopy from the alcohol and didn't know what was coming out of his mouth. He made one crude joke after another and gave Joanie a couple of *titty-twisters* for good measure.

When the two men got tired of dancing with the women, they came over to me and started a conversation.

"How would you like a dance, kid?" Mary asked, smelling of alcohol.

Once my uncle noticed Mary and Peg talking to me, he came over and whispered in my ear, "Don't listen to those hags. They spread rumors about every man that turns them down. Next thing you know, they're going to spread some crap about you."

"He's with me," my uncle said, and the women got the message that I was too young and off-limits.

I looked up at the TV screen. "God, the Phillies suck," I muttered. They were losing 10 to 2.

24

I had a series of dreams that my father was dead shortly after those barflies at the Falcon Club told me that he swung both ways.

In one dream, I could never get close enough to the casket to touch his hand or to feel his cold forehead because of all the hovering people. They were all his friends and customers.

People who loved and worshipped the ground he walked on wouldn't let me get to the casket to pay my respects.

Another dream was a series of flashbacks. I was sitting on Dad's lap and rubbing his bald head. I wanted to impress him, so I grabbed my Richie Ashburn glove, and we tossed a baseball in the backyard. He caught my fastest pitch and threw it back as a curveball that had good movement. When we got tired of having a catch, we walked to Castor Avenue to get a pizza at Dante's Inferno. We didn't stop eating because we never got satisfied. We kept asking for more slices, more hot peppers, and parmigiana cheese. We still weren't satisfied, so we drove down to Pat's Steaks and ordered two big cheesesteaks. We ate them standing up at the counter like the tough guys did.

In all my dreams about my father, not once did I see him with another man. Only me, his son, having fun, and he was always the hero.

He was a hero regardless of how many stolen bushels of Italian peppers he accepted from thieving scoundrels. He was a hero despite the number of skanky whores or men he bonked. It didn't matter that dozens of porn magazines were in the tiles of our drop ceiling. Sure, he paid Mafioso protection money in the form of produce, Italian cold cuts, provolone, and gallon containers of imported olive oil—but who cared about all that stuff? None of that mattered.

I loved him anyway.

I had to forgive him for lying to me because life was short. I knew he would die eventually, and I didn't want any anger between us.

Grandma always told me how cute my father was, a beautiful blond-haired boy growing up in the brutal winters of Northeastern Pennsylvania, shivering in his poverty, and selling Hershey bars on the street corners. While his father, Grandpa Izzy, was getting drunk, Grandma was busy making ends meet and never had time to show my father any affection, so he had to fend for himself. He had to find the love he needed in other people, male or female. Dad just wanted to be loved.

As I leafed through all his Army pictures, I could see him with his male friends going to Amsterdam, Italy, and France. I could see him smiling in front of the Eiffel Tower and leaning to the right with the Tower of Pisa. I realized that there was so much to know about my father that I will never understand and that all of those little personal things that irritated me about him were his business.

I realized that my relationship with my father would never be perfect, that all his secrets and love interests would be in a book that I would never read. And that was okay.

"Everything in life doesn't have to be tied in a nice little ribbon," Grandma said.

I had to stop hating my father and love him the way Grandma did.

25

Near the end of the summer, Aunt Mary and I picked up Grandma in Philly and spent a week at the Jersey shore. Uncle Leo stayed in Pottsville because he said it was the busiest time of year for selling fruit and that he didn't like the beach because there was too much damn sand, and it gets into his underwear.

Aunt Mary said, "No use worrying about Uncle Leo. He can take care of himself." But I knew that she would rather have him here no matter what sarcastic things she said about him.

We stayed at the Chelsea Hotel like we always did, two blocks from the boardwalk on Chelsea Avenue. An old Atlantic City Victorian with about ten rooms and a big wooden porch with a couple of rockers. The room had a fresh ocean breeze coming through our open windows, blowing the drapes. We felt the energy of the vacationers scrambling to the beach, excited to be a part of the bustling atmosphere that so many people enjoyed after a long winter. We loved walking the boards, the sound of a thousand feet stomping, and making the wood creak and buckle was music to our ears. My lungs and the ocean were a good match. The salty air always made me breathe better.

We strolled by the Mayflower and the Breakers hotels, watched the tawny-skinned men push the rolling chairs for people who got tired of walking. We smelled the freshly fried donuts, sampled some roasted Planter's peanuts, and had pink cotton candy followed by a funnel cake with plenty of powdered sugar.

Grandma took a seat facing the ocean to rest her gnarly feet, while Aunt Mary and I played Skee-Ball in the arcades, racking up hundreds of coupon tickets. I got enough coupons to buy a box of Candy Lips and a couple of jumbo jawbreakers that I swore cracked a couple of my molars. We rode the snaking roller coaster and got dizzy at the top of the Ferris wheel. We went to Steel Pier and saw the monkey playing a music box in the large glass case. Later, we all watched in awe as the lady on the white horse dove sixty-feet into a massive pool of water and galloped out like there was no problem.

"How does the horse do that without getting hurt?" I asked.

"I guess the horse is not afraid of water," Grandma answered. "He must be a seahorse."

She was the only one who laughed at the joke, but I thought it was funny.

"Maybe horses are not afraid of things like we are," I said, "that's why they're able to do scary things."

I remember when I first came down the shore with Aunt Mary. I was afraid of the waves even though they were only a couple of feet tall. Uncle Leo came with us at that time. He took a picture of me with my bloated belly running away from the waves as they crashed ashore.

"Here comes one," Aunt Mary said.

"Oh, boy," and I jumped as high as I could.

"Don't worry, I'm holding you," Aunt Mary said, and we jumped another swelling wave together. We bounced over each one and watched them roll past us to shore. The foamy water had strands of seaweed that stuck to our hair. The saltwater ran up our noses and tickled. We laughed and blew out snot bubbles.

Looking out into the Atlantic Ocean as a teenager, I thought of how quickly summer comes and goes, how the years pass, and you don't realize how short life is and, just as quickly, you aren't down Atlantic City anymore walking the beach and collecting shells with your favorite aunt. Life rushes past you like a giant wave. Vacations with Aunt Mary and Grandma felt so temporary, just as they were beginning, they seemed to end far too soon. But we always made the best of the few days at the beach. We stayed in the water as long as we could and ate the foods that we craved for all winter, even though some of the fried seafood made our bellies ache and gave us the runs. At the Shore, we forgot about our troubles—Grandma forgot about her bad ticker, I forgot about my asthmatic lungs, and, of course, Aunt Mary forgot that Uncle Leo was a drunk and a scoundrel. When we were on the sand surrounded by the blue sky and vast ocean, we focused on how nice it felt. We seemed to morph with the curling, cresting waters; the blue-gray ocean held us up and shook our bodies like a Waring blender. In the sea, I realized that each wave was a new opportunity to wash clean all my sins and misbehaviors. Each wave was a perfect moment to forget about our troubles and just to focus on the present. Nothing bad ever happens to you when you are jumping waves or walking the boards with people you love.

Aunt Mary and I ran out of the water and sat on our beach towels while Grandma lounged on her comfy folding chair with a floppy straw hat and big sunglasses. We watched the tide roll in and out as the enormous orange sunset on the horizon. We listened to the cacophony of voices on the boardwalk—the seagulls squealing and barking like dogs in the sky. The Ferris wheel kept turning like the planet we were on. No matter how many times people rode the rollercoaster, they always screamed and hollered like it was their first time. Every season was the same but different. There would be a new set of handsome boys who made cute girls giggle and a new flock of sea birds flying above us in unison as if they were trained jet pilots.

We walked carefully in our flip-flops back to the hotel to shower off the sticky sand that stuck to our joyful bodies. Later we ate fried shrimp, crab cakes, French fries, and finished it off with a scoop of vanilla ice cream on top of a slice of pecan pie. As usual, my Grandma took a few knives and forks and stuffed them in her big red purse when the waiter wasn't looking. All I could do was shake my head. I knew that I could never go back to stealing or any of the other stupid stuff that I used to do with Padidas and Bergman. I knew that I didn't want to grow up and become like my father or Uncle Leo. I was determined to stay out of trouble.

26

"Hey, let's see a movie," Aunt Mary suggested. "It's our last day here."

"No thanks, there's nothing playing that I like," said Grandma, whose gout was probably acting up from all the fried foods. After a big dinner, she usually went back to the room and took a big swig of Pepto Bismol from the bottle and propped her feet on the bed.

"How about *The Graduate*," I suggested, knowing that Aunt Mary would say yes.

Grandma walked gingerly back to the hotel, and we saw *The Graduate* without her. We watched Mrs. Robinson throw the keys into Benjamin's tropical fish tank and watched her seduce him. Benjamin would later have sex with Mrs. Robinson at a local Beverly Hills hotel and then fall in love with her daughter, Elaine. His little red sports car with the stick shift was so cool that I imagined myself driving it down the highway as if it were mine.

Once I saw Elaine's long hair, I thought about Sandy Finkle. Her eyes were big and brown. Sandy was tall and skinny and had a little mole on the right side of her cheek. I was short like Benjamin, so it gave me hope that I could have a beautiful girl someday. God, I wished that Sandy could see how mature I was.

I wish she would knock on my door at night while I was sleeping and say, "I've changed my mind, Harry. I think I want to be your girlfriend. You're so cool for a short guy."

"I love you, Sandy," I would say and hop into my sleek red sports car, and we'd drive away down the coast into oblivion.

Aunt Mary was on her second bag of popcorn as Elaine left for Berkley, and Benjamin followed her in his Alfa Romeo, totally convinced that she would agree to marry him even though he had bonked her mother about a thousand times.

"Could you believe the nerve of this guy, Aunt Mary?"

If I knew Sandy loved me, I would drive from the Jersey shore to Philly right now. That's if I had my license and had a car that looked as sharp as Benjamin's.

"No, I can't, Harry. Benjamin's out of his mind for going after her. It's clear she doesn't want to have anything to do with him."

"He just can't take no for an answer, Aunt Mary. He's determined. Don't you admire that?"

My aunt didn't answer. She stuck her hand back and forth from the popcorn to her mouth in a nice, easy rhythm.

Benjamin drove down the Pacific Coast Highway like a madman, much like my Uncle Leo does when he's toasted and coming home from a bar in the middle of the night, except that Uncle Leo drives drunk, goes through stop signs and hits parked cars.

At one point in the movie, I got up for more buttered popcorn and a big box of Goobers. When I came back, Elaine intended to marry another guy. Some strait-laced jerk that smoked a pipe and was going to medical school—a real loser. You could tell that Elaine was just doing it to please her parents. Marrying someone who could buy her a big house in Beverly Hills was no reason to get married.

"What's with Elaine?" I asked Aunt Mary, who was now munching on a handful of M&M's between fistfuls of popcorn.

"She's as stupid as Benjamin."

"Yeah, she's marrying a stupid doctor, someone that she thinks her family will like."

"This movie is strange, isn't it?" Aunt Mary commented.

She was used to watching old black-and-white flicks where the characters were dignified and sensible like Cary Grant and Katharine Hepburn. She loved films where violins and harps played in the background and not a couple of hippie folk singers like Simon and Garfunkel.

"I could care less about what my mother and father thought. If I wanted to marry Sandy, I wouldn't even ask them if it was okay. They'd either come to my wedding, or screw them."

Benjamin was beating everyone with a gigantic crucifix like Jesus probably did to the money lenders back in his day. He grabbed Elaine and took her out of the church as if he were Zorro rescuing a beautiful Spanish damsel. They hopped a bus to who knows where and sat in the backseat of that dirty, grimy bus. She was in her beautiful white wedding gown with those gorgeous brown eyes, and he looked like he was mugged.

In the end, it was confusing. Once Elaine and Benjamin were in the back seat, they looked at each other kind of funny, like "What did we just do? Where do we go from here?"

"What the hell happened?" I asked Aunt Mary, looking for guidance.

"I think they both fucked-up if you ask me. Excuse my French, Harry."

"I hope it works out. Benjamin tried so hard to get her. It would be a shame if they didn't have a future."

"I wouldn't be surprised if it didn't work out, Harry. Guys don't know what they want sometimes. Once they get it, the challenge is over, and they go out and look for something that they think is better."

"Sounds like Uncle Sy, always buying new cars."

I untangled a knot from my longish brown hair and finished my box of Goobers. Aunt Mary was usually right about such things. But I know for a fact that I would never get tired of Sandy or cheat on her like Uncle Leo did with Aunt Mary, or my dad did with my mother.

On the way back to the hotel, Aunt Mary gave me a few bucks, and I stopped at a record store to pick up the soundtrack to *The Graduate*. It was like buying something divinely inspired, music from the heavens. It was the cherry on top of this wonderful vacation.

"Thanks, Aunt Mary," I said as I quickly unwrapped the cellophane from the record jacket.

Aunt Mary couldn't have children, so I was the next best thing. I loved her because she did things for me that my parents were incapable of doing. She took me places and bought me trendy clothing like a Nehru jacket and a groovy pair of Dingo boots, even if they were two sizes too big.

Aunt Mary felt sorry for me because my mother was in the mental hospital and wasn't coming out any time soon. During the summers that I spent with her, she wanted to compensate for my mother's lack of presence in my life. Aunt Mary wanted to be the rock, the female role model that I sorely needed. She gave me all the love and attention that her chubby body could muster.

As we walked along the boardwalk, I asked Aunt Mary something. "If Grandma dies, and I'm not saying she will right away, could I live with you? I wouldn't take up much space, and I'd help around the house."

Aunt Mary's eyes lit up. "Of course, you can, honey. You know you're always welcome. Uncle Leo and I would love that very much."

"One of these days, I don't think Grandma's medicine is going to work."

"Don't worry, Harry. When Grandma dies, Uncle Leo and I will handle it. We'll drive right down to Philly, pick you up, and take care of everything."

27

Grandma and Aunt Mary slept in the big bed, and I was on the cot with the coiled springs sticking in my ribs. I also had two foam pillows that the hotel people gave me along with a non-woolen blanket because of my allergies to wool and feathers.

The uncomfortable cot didn't deter me from my paradise. I'll always remember the nights down the shore. The quiet noise. The flashing lights from the pier. The sounds of the crashing waves in the distance. The murmur of people on the boardwalk and the fresh salty air was coming through the windows ruffling the curtains. You didn't need an air conditioner there, nor a fan, just an open window cooling your moist skin. It was so damn comfortable that I couldn't stand it. I just wanted to stay awake and feel the sweetness of the evening air. I would bundle up in my fresh sheets and non-woolen blanket like a mummy and imagine sleeping on the beach. I could just die here, but I knew I wouldn't die. Not just yet, anyway. My lungs were working so smoothly that you'd hardly know that I had asthma. Only the pleasant bellowing in and out, breath flowing joyfully through my lungs without any complications, the way God intended.

Meanwhile, Aunt Mary and Grandma Edna exchanged choking snores while I shut my eyes and slept like a baby throughout the night, not getting up once to take a pee.

28

The next morning, we packed our bags and squeezed them into the trunk of Aunt Mary's light blue Ford Fairlane. We left the ice-cream cones, funnel cakes, and fried donuts behind. The ocean waves were in our rearview mirror as we headed back to Pottsville, to the boondocks of the Schuylkill Valley. We took the turnpike exit for Pennsylvania. We were on our way back to a place that never seemed to change. I unwrapped a Black Cow and looked at the album cover of Simon and Garfunkel's *The Graduate*. I stared at Mrs. Robinson's sexy legs as she removed her stockings in front of the mortified Benjamin Braddock. I imagined what Benjamin must have been experiencing when he did it for the first time in that Beverly Hills hotel room, how he was so nervous and, at the same time, how proud he must have been for himself. Grandma was in the back seat peeling the wrapper from a Baby Jane and putting a couple in her mouth. I wondered if she hocked it from the candy store that she went to on the boardwalk. Grandma was happy, though, had a good few days of rest, which was healthy for her heart. Aunt Mary had both hands on the steering wheel, and I never had any fears when she was driving. She turned up Roger Miller's *King of the Road* on the radio, Uncle Leo's favorite song, as she grabbed a handful of Wise Potato Chips and stuck them all in her mouth. She was in a hurry to get back home. So was I.

Crazy Grandpa

If there was ever a son of a bitch, it was Grandpa Izzy. He would tell you that to your face if you were bold enough to ask. Even in his seventies, he was tough. He had a big round head like a watermelon and a wide body like an old Pottsville Maroon football player. He'd sit on his favorite reclining chair smoking a stogie, dressed in his work clothes with an old pair of Oxfords without laces.

He sent me to Smokey's to pick up a box of Conastogas. It didn't matter if I was too young to buy cigars or that I didn't feel like walking up a steep hill. He'd call me a "lazy little fucker" and raise his wooden cane if I refused. He was proud of that cane—said he got it from a blind Indian from Tamaqua who carved tree branches into walking sticks.

"Here," he'd wave a dollar. "You can get a bottle of pop for yourself."

He knew I bribed easily, but I would have gotten it anyway. He was my buddy in an odd sort of way. We were in the same boat. He never had much of a family and neither did I. We were "comrades of abandonment."

When we were watching old black-and-white movies he'd say, "I know that guy. I used to play darts with him at the Falcon Club." I smiled and thought, *there's no way he knows Gregory Peck.*

When he sat on the porch on an old wooden rocker that creaked every time he rocked, he'd shake his cane at the kids riding by on their bikes. I liked watching their scared little faces as they pedaled as fast as they could back to their mommas. These were the same kids who didn't want to play kickball with me because I was a city kid and they thought all city kids were devils from hell.

An irate parent came to our house once and threatened to call the cops. Grandpa Izzy stood up as straight as his old body would allow and took a giant swing at her and barely missed. When Aunt Mary heard the commotion, she hurried outside. "He has hardening of the arteries and he's senile," she explained to the woman. "I'm sorry, he doesn't know any better."

The woman told Aunt Mary that she had a relative with dementia, "But the next time something like this happens," she said, "I'm calling the police."

"Go ahead and call the cops, you ole battle axe!" Grandpa huffed. The lady just ignored him and walked away.

He always got the last word in.

"Come on *kadiddlehopper*—we're going for a ride!"

He drove my uncle's old Studebaker with a stick on the column, plush foamy seats, and faux wooden accents on the dash. It was an old car but solid like a tank. And he was the perfect lunatic to drive it.

I was only nine years old. I didn't know that Grandpa drove like a maniac. It didn't matter if he had dementia or was a chronic alcoholic. I would have taken a ride in a helicopter if he had one.

Grandpa didn't use his turn signals and never came to a complete stop at a traffic light, but I trusted him with my life. I loved Grandpa's crazy behavior. There was something about his cocky, brash attitude that I admired. He might have hated Aunt Mary and most of the universe, but I knew he liked me even though he didn't always show it.

"Son of a bitch!" he hollered at an old lady pushing an overstuffed shopping cart while walking across Second Street.

He showed no mercy.

He wanted people to know that he was no chump. His

attitude of distrust reflected his homeless years when he lived in a cardboard box on Minersville Street and when countless people teased him unmercifully and threw empty beer bottles at him. When Grandma kicked him out of the house forty years ago, he never recovered. He quit working, stopped taking care of himself and became a *hobo,* as Grandma called it.

"Go fuck yourself!" he shouted to a guy who blew his horn at him for going through a red light.

Grandpa wasn't afraid of anyone—not even the police. Surprisingly, he was never pulled over by the police or got arrested. "The cops in Pottsville love me because they're just as bad as me," he used to say.

He took a drag from his stogie and wiped the sweat off his brow with his red and white handkerchief that had been used too many times.

He laughed and flicked the ashes from my hair.

"Sorry, Buddy," he said. "It's hard driving and looking where ashes are falling."

He was happy when he had a little booze in him, often keeping a pint of whiskey hidden under the seat when he got thirsty. And he seemed to get thirsty a lot, finishing one bottle and going to the liquor store for another.

He often drove down Laurel Boulevard, pointing out people that he thought he knew. "See that guy, that's my friend from the Dusslefink. And that guy with the gray Fedora used to play poker with me every Friday night. I used to take the shirt off his back most nights."

I knew it was bullshit but I wanted to believe him.

"That's where my Poppy bought me my first pint of ale," he said proudly, pointing to the Yuengling Brewery on Mahantongo Street.

He talked about Pottsville like he owned it, like he knew every person who ever lived there. He was proud of his little hillbilly town and its slow moving, working class vibe. He often said that everything in Pottsville is the way it's supposed to be and he wouldn't change a thing.

When my Grandpa got hungry, he'd take me to the Garfield Diner even if he didn't have a cent on him. He treated me to a hot roast beef sandwich covered in brown gravy with a side of mashed potatoes.

"Hello, Izzy," said an old waitress named Verlie. "What have you been up to, ya big lug?" She bent over the counter with her big boobs popping out and poured Grandpa a cup of extra black coffee just the way he liked it. "Who's the kid?" she asked while snapping open a bottle of Coke and then put it in front of me.

"That's my little *kadiddlehopper*," he announced loud enough so everyone in the diner could hear.

"Fine looking boy," she told Grandpa Izzy. "He doesn't look anything like you."

After I finished my hot roast beef, the waitress brought me the biggest banana split I ever saw with the whipped cream about a foot tall.

"This one's on the house," she said. "Your Grandpa's a good man, crazy as hell, but a genuine guy."

I couldn't eat the banana split fast enough.

Aunt Mary broke the bad news at dinnertime. She didn't want me to drive with Grandpa anymore.

"It's too dangerous," she said. "He shouldn't be allowed to drive anyway. His eyes are bad and he doesn't follow any traffic laws."

My uncle looked up from his plate of knockwurst and sauerkraut. "Let the boy go with him if he wants. It'll teach him how *not* to drive."

"That's not funny, Leo! The man doesn't have a license."

"This is Pottsville," my uncle said as if to insinuate that Grandpa's not the only one driving without a license.

Uncle Leo was not such a good driver, either. He must have taken lessons from Grandpa because he had a glove compartment full of unpaid parking tickets and his pick-up had quite a few dents.

Aunt Mary looked at me. "Maybe you should hang around with kids your own age. Go out and have some fun."

"I don't know anyone around here, Aunt Mary. All the kids I know don't like me because I'm from Philly."

The truth was that all the neighborhood kids were boring compared to Grandpa. He and I secretly left the house each morning in my uncle's Studebaker. He'd often let me steer while he had a stogie in his mouth, a quart of beer in a brown paper bag, and his cane halfway out the window. We laughed, cursed at annoying strangers, and made fun of random people like the bad-asses that we thought we were. In the back of our minds, we knew our joy rides wouldn't last forever.

Things got worse for Grandpa in the next year.

When Aunt Mary fell asleep on the sofa one night while waiting up for Uncle Leo to come home, Grandpa hobbled down the stairs wearing only his white T-shirt. He stood in front of his sleeping daughter-in-law and began to rub himself and groan like a horny dog. She woke up and was horrified to see Grandpa's old gray pecker dangling in front of her face like a tarantula about to sting her.

She jumped up and ran to the kitchen, grabbed a carving knife, and went after poor Grandpa who hadn't the slightest clue what he did wrong. When she looked at his scared face, she thought better about it, "Get the hell upstairs you old son of a bitch!"

That was the last straw for Aunt Mary who never wanted to take in Grandpa in the first place.

Uncle Leo stumbled through the door a few hours later, and Aunt Mary got in his face. She told him that if he didn't get his father out of there soon, she was going to leave.

I didn't know where Grandpa would go. I remembered once they tried to get him into a nursing home but he messed up the interview by threatening to punch the director in the face because he reminded him of a guy who teased him when he was homeless. The sad truth was that nobody wanted an old man who was as brash and ill-tempered as Grandpa.

Grandpa told me that in 1894, his pregnant mother came to Ellis Island in a big ship with a boat full of other Russian immigrants. He said he was born on that ship when the Chinese flag was up. "That makes me Chinese," Grandpa laughed.

I knew he wasn't Chinese and that he wasn't born on the boat but I loved listening to his stories.

"When did you meet Grandma Edna?" I asked.

"I met her in Pottsville in 1918. She was working at her grandfather's variety store called Greenburn's. She had bright red hair like Lucille Ball and shiny white teeth. I couldn't keep my eyes off her."

Grandpa usually paused when he told stories because he would lose his train of thought.

"She didn't like me at first, but I had to have her." And he waved his cane high in the air like he was the music man.

"How did you manage to get her to like you?"

"I wore her down, kid. She was so tired of me bothering her at work that she finally agreed to go out."

"Where did you take her?"

"We went to a club to see Tommy Dorsey. She was impressed and thought I was loaded. Little did she know that I was a pauper, a junk dealer in them days."

Grandpa laughed, bringing up some phlegm in the process.

"Used to have a horse-and-buggy back then and loaded it up with metals to sell to factories. It was a lot of work to make a few bucks, but I got by.

"She always thought I wasn't good enough. She wanted to change me. Told me not to go to saloons or hang out with my cronies who played poker. She wanted me to stop selling junk, too. I just couldn't do it." He wiped his runny nose on his sleeve.

"She got mad and kicked me to the streets with nothing but an old alligator suitcase and a few bucks in my pocket."

That was one of the rare occasions when Grandpa told me about his life. He was either cursing or too angry to get to know. When he opened up, I felt his pain and sorrow and saw the person that he really was. The callouses on his hands and feet reflected his hard life, and things would get even harder.

Uncle Leo went into Grandpa's room, a forbidden place for most people. The room smelled of alcohol, urine, and dirty clothes. The linoleum floor was spotted with poop streaks and dried spit. His shoes and pants were crammed in the same dresser drawer. Only when Grandpa was out of the house, could Aunt Mary go into this forbidden place to mop and sanitize the room with bleach.

"You're gonna have to move out, Pop. You can't live here anymore." I knew it was difficult for my uncle, but Aunt Mary couldn't deal with Grandpa anymore. Her psoriasis was acting up something awful, red patches all over her back and elbows.

"I didn't touch her cat!" Grandpa hollered. "All of a sudden your wife says I killed her cat."

"Start packing, you're going to the Davis Hotel, Pop."

"Like hell I am!" Grandpa shouted, and waved his cane at Uncle Leo.

The next thing I knew, Uncle Leo stumbled down the steps holding his nose, blood dripping everywhere on the creaky wooden stairs.

"He's getting the *fuck* out of here tonight," he told Aunt Mary when he got to the bottom of the stairs. She quickly got a towel to stop the bleeding, and then she drove Uncle Leo to the hospital emergency room.

Uncle Leo loved his father despite Grandpa being a lifelong drunk and never showing him much attention or love. It wasn't easy for Uncle Leo to drop off Grandpa at a hotel in the middle of the night and leave him all alone. But there was really no other choice. Grandpa Izzy was getting more dangerous and unpredictable.

* * *

As it turned out, Grandpa did okay for the next couple of years at the Davis Hotel. He could sleep on the dirty sheets with his shoes on, stuff his filthy underwear in the drawers, and walk around naked in his room if he didn't have the window shades up. He could be as crazy as he wanted and no one would ever know.

Drinking eventually caught up with him, though. One afternoon he tumbled down the stairs after losing his grip on the bannister, breaking his hip and having a heart attack at the same time. The ambulance people said that his heart stopped temporarily but, lucky for him, it started up again when they administered CPR. They said they found him on the floor with a smile on his face, alcohol on his breath, and a stogie nub in his mouth. His broken cane lay beside his broken body, but he didn't seem to give a damn. He was seventy-eight and still alive.

Before we finally got Grandpa Izzy into a nursing home, Aunt Mary and I would often stop at the Davis Hotel and see him sitting on a folding chair with his friends Rusty and Johnson. They were both old drunks like him who reminisced about their bar fights and the women they almost had the opportunity to sleep with.

I'd wave to him and shout, "Hey Grandpa!"

He always seemed happy to see me. I couldn't help thinking about the times when we drove around Pottsville doing anything we pleased, breaking traffic laws, and shouting at people with no thought to how much trouble we might cause. I kept an old picture of him on my dresser holding me in his arms as a little baby, right next to my Uncle Leo's Studebaker. He was much younger then and happier, too.

Aunt Mary never said hello to Grandpa. She parked the car around the corner and I walked over to him carrying a pack of clean underwear and socks. He proudly introduced me to his friends, "This is my grandson," he said with a wide, toothless grin. "He's a goddamn *kadiddlehopper!*"

His friends would say that I was a fine looking boy and asked me why I had so much hair and Grandpa so little.

He'd take a drag from his stogie, run his hand over his bare scalp, and just laugh.

Hazleton by Noon

The window of the truck was open a crack to let in some cool night air. It felt good since Dad had the defroster on high and we were wrapped up in our heavy coats and long johns. The weatherman on the radio said that Philly could get up to twelve inches and the northern regions of the state might get as much as three feet. But it didn't bother Dad. He had chains on his tires, and he knew how to drive in the snow.

It felt good to be with Dad even though the only time I could spend with him was when he was driving a truck. He worked all the time and most nights he came home when I was in bed. He never took me to the movies or to have a catch like the other dads. Mom always had to take up the slack, or I would hang out with my friends.

As we made our way onto the I-95 ramp, Dad turned the dial to hear a country song. He seemed happy when he listened to the old singers like Merle Haggard and Johnny Cash. It was as if they were talking his lingo, the words of the blue collar worker. He was a truck driver through and through, and those country harmonies meant something special to him.

We passed the South Philly sports complex where the Eagles and Sixers play, finally getting off at the Penrose exit to the Food Distribution Center.

We stopped at a light where the homeless men huddled by a burning trash can trying to keep warm. A tall man wearing a Fantucci's Fish Market hoodie with tattered work gloves recognized Dad and came over to our truck. "I haven't seen you in a long time, Mel."

"Yep," Dad said. "My business partner died. Had to take off for a while to settle some legal things."

"Glad to see ya back. Need help loadin' your truck?"

"My son's going to be my assistant today, Sully. Maybe next time."

The man looked disappointed as if he had just been robbed of money that was rightfully his.

"If ya need me—ya know where I am," and the poor man took his place in the circle around the burning trash can.

As we drove off, Dad told me that the man's name was Sullivan, Sully for short, and that he was a royal pain in the ass. But he seemed nice enough to me. Dad often put people down who appeared a little different than normal.

"Don't get me wrong, Sully tries, but I can't let him stack the truck by himself anymore—he'll jack it up."

Dad was a stickler when it came to loading a produce truck. He was the best truck and cooler stacker around and made sure that he didn't waste any space in the trailer. "Every box has its place," he always said as if the boxes and crates were people.

When we entered the Food Center, it was like experiencing an X-rated Land of Oz. There were hordes of all races and nationalities who used obscene language and profane gestures pushing hand trucks, lifting heavy boxes, and backing 18-wheelers into narrow loading docks. Dad seemed to enjoy the banter and had no trouble dishing it out.

"How the hell are you, Mel? Sorry to hear about your partner. Give my condolences to the family."

"Will do," said Dad leafing through his small notepad.

"We just got in a shipment of bananas, Mel. A little green right now, but they'll ripen in a few days."

"No, not this time, Tony. I got a surplus in the store that I can't get rid of."

We walked the cement platform of the outdoor food center, checking over the merchandise while trying to ignore most of the

South Philly wise guy chatter. A stocky man with a Phillies cap motioned my Dad to a stall with a load of vine-ripe tomatoes.

"I've got a good deal for you, Mel."

Dad winked at me as if to say, *watch this*. I observed him haggle for about twenty minutes, back and forth, until the man reluctantly reduced the price. "I know how to talk to these wise guys," he said proudly. He loved it when he could show off his bargaining skills. He learned it from his father who used to come to the market in a '55 Chevy pickup with a big, fat cigar in his mouth and a bald head shining like the afternoon sun.

Dad had an endless amount of energy even in the frigid early morning when the rest of the world was bundled up in bed. He went from one stall to the next, bargaining and bickering with every salesman like a smooth-talking machine.

"Take your crap and stick it!" Dad shouted and walked away like he was frustrated.

"Don't be a prick, Mel. I'm not making anything on them."

"Asshole."

"Numb nuts."

They'd curse each other in the worst way imaginable for ten minutes, acting as if they'd come to fisticuffs, and then hug each other like they were long lost brothers.

"Matty, you're one greedy son-of-a-bitch."

"Bite on this, Mel," the guy said holding his crotch.

Dad loved the place. It was the only time I ever saw him happy. Life outside of the produce business was boring for him. He seemed lost as a father and a husband. But give him a bushel of peppers or a crate of California cantaloupes to sell, and he'd know what to do with it.

"It's sure good to be back," he said, smiling and rubbing my shaggy brown hair like a sheepdog. "I didn't realize how much I missed these sons-of-bitches."

I guess I was too young to appreciate this place. I found the Food Center confusing and crude. Grown men acted like bullies but who would change their colors on a dime and embrace each other after cursing and acting verbally abusive. I knew that when I grew up, I wouldn't choose this kind of job. I was too sensitive, didn't have a thick enough skin for this line of work. I wanted a job where people started their day at a reasonable hour and didn't use four-letter words in every sentence. I wanted a future where my whole life wasn't wrapped up in the price of a box of Florida oranges. I planned on getting a regular job where I could come home to a family that I cared about, and I would know how to be a good father to my kids and wouldn't ignore my wife when she talked to me.

When Dad finally decided that he had everything that he came for, he began to load the truck. It was always a well-calculated process. He crisscrossed the heavy bags of potatoes like a square pyramid. He placed each box, basket, and crate of produce in the right spot, one on top of the other, airtight and utilizing every bit of space in the truck. I pulled the fruit with a pallet jack, and he stacked the merchandise, loading it to the brim.

By the time we finished, the snow had started to come down heavier.

"Got to get to Hazleton by noon," Dad repeated. "The customers will be waiting for us. And I sure don't want to lose any business today after being off for a while."

I remembered a couple of years ago when we had a tough time getting up the Blue Mountain in the snow, but I didn't say anything. We were stuck for a couple of hours; had to empty the truck and dig ourselves out of three feet of heavy, wet snow. We spent hours shoveling, our hands were red and swollen from the cold despite wearing gloves. I still get a shiver up my spine just thinking about that day.

Dad locked the backend of the truck, and pulled over to a little food shack. We had an egg sandwich on toast and shared some home fries to hold us over for the long trip ahead.

"I still can't believe how well you stacked that truck, Dad."

He smiled and rubbed my brown mop of hair again. That was two head rubs in one day. I couldn't remember my father showing me that much physical affection twice in one day. It was a minor miracle.

"That's what happens when you've been in the business for thirty years, son. But don't you be a produce man. Go to college and make something of yourself."

I nodded and had every intention of doing so.

My father was a good man despite all of his bad habits. He just grew up in the wrong family with an alcoholic father who was a workaholic and a mother who was always more concerned with her appearance than caring for her two sons.

Sully knocked on the window and rubbed his hands together. He asked Dad if he could borrow ten dollars for food and promised to load the truck for free next week.

Dad didn't hesitate. He reached into his back pocket, pulled out an overstuffed wallet and gave Sully a twenty. "Buy yourself something nice," and Sully took the money as if he had just won the lottery.

"We better get moving," Dad said, looking at the little hands on his Timex.

He turned the key. The big engine rumbled and bucked like it was about to stall out. He grabbed the shifter and did a zig-zag and slipped it into the right gear. The engine settled down into a manageable hum, and we were on our way.

I opened my window just a crack. The winter sun peeked out from the snow clouds. Big snowflakes hit the heated windshield and melted as we made our way down the interstate highway heading north. There were more cars on the road even though the streets were mushy and slick. People were going to their regular nine-to-five jobs while our day had long since started. I was tired, and was surprised that Dad offered me his lap to rest my head on. I could hear the truck's powerful engine grinding when he changed gears, feeling each bump in the road, and hearing the soothing country music playing on the radio. Something told me that we would have no trouble making it up Blue Mountain.

Under the Suburban Sky

As I rode in my Uncle Sy's new Eldorado Cadillac, I kept looking out the window and wondering how I was going to deal with such a control freak.

We drove by the sea of row homes, past the shabby gas stations, the cheap chicken shacks, and the cheesesteak shops that always claimed that they were the best in the city.

"I used to live on that block," my uncle bragged about one of the rundown streets of row homes. "It looks like a ghetto now. They don't know how to take care of things."

Uncle Sy claimed to be a good man but he was prejudiced against the poor. I didn't want to hear what he had to say about people who didn't have as much money as he had, so I leaned over and turned up the radio. He gave me a scowl, but it didn't stop him. He continued to rant about how people shouldn't make excuses for their poverty, like bad luck or having lousy parents. "They have to pick themselves up by their bootstraps, just like I did."

We drove past the Philadelphia Zoo and turned onto the City Avenue ramp. These were my uncle's people. People with high paying professions, like doctors and lawyers, who lived in big stone mansions with high hedges and drove cars that seemed to purr with power instead of old clunkers that coughed up fumes.

My uncle bragged about his expensive suits and fancy Italian wingtips. He said he had his own private tailor who made his suits fit perfectly.

"Why buy cheap clothing when you can afford the very best?" he said waiting for me to agree with him. Instead, I stared out the window in silence.

I knew I was getting closer to his house when I could see the high wooden fences and the thick green hedges that hid the homes. We pulled into his gravel-filled driveway and entered his big, sprawling brick-and-stone house with a huge wooden double door at the entrance. It was like entering a mausoleum.

Aunt Joyce greeted me at the door and gave me a hug that lacked enthusiasm, "Harry, it's so nice that you could get away from the noisy city."

I hugged her back and said, "It's not that bad, Aunt Joyce."

She was a snob, too, who grew up in Wayne and thought that everyone should be as privileged and entitled as she was. She didn't understand why people were poor. Like my uncle, she thought it was a moral defect or an abnormality from a bad pregnancy.

"Boys," Uncle Sy called his sons as if they were bellhops at a swanky hotel. "Please, take Harry's stuff to his room."

Joel grabbed my duffle bag. He was the oldest and, after years of lifting weights, was a bodybuilder. He was also the starting quarterback for his high school football team and had a scholarship to Bowling Green. Uncle Sy talked about him like he was going to be another Bob Griese.

I unpacked my clothes. I knew that I had to stack everything correctly in the dresser drawer or my anal uncle would say I was a slob and tell my grandmother when I got home.

"When you're in my house, you do things my way," he'd say, but in my mind, I had already planned to break some of his precious rules.

The son of a bitch bought me a Bulova watch for Christmas, so I could keep track of his nutty agenda when I came over his house. He taped the schedule to my door. At 11 a.m., there was a boring roundtable in the living room. At noon we had lunch. He was so anal that he wrote down what we were going to eat like some restaurant—*tuna salad on rye with chips and sweet pickles*. Big whoop!

I quickly put my duffle bag into the closet, made sure my sneakers were tied, and my shirt wasn't hanging out of my pants. By the time I got to the living room, Uncle Sy and his family were already talking about some school activity as if it were high priority, top secret stuff.

"Structure," he kept emphasizing as if it were a magical word. "You got to have structure in your life or you won't amount to anything. That's what I learned in the Army. That's what I'm going to drill into your heads if it's the last thing I do."

Uncle Sy was a man who had everything. He was tall, handsome, and had pearly white teeth. He was rich as hell, and a war hero to boot. He never let anyone forget that he earned a Purple Heart from the Korean War, which was the first thing he showed anybody when they walked in the house. "The war was tough," he said, "but I came out of it like a man. Everyone should have to serve in the Army if you ask me."

If you ask me, the Army had screwed him up. He was probably a reasonable guy before he went in.

Even his kids were brainwashed by his bull. They cowered to him worse than some beaten-down stray dogs I knew in Philly. Joel told his father his schedule for football practice, and Eric handed him a paper to sign for basketball tryouts. I just sat on one of his gaudy velvet chairs looking up at the high ceiling with its brown wooden beams. There wasn't anything for me to announce except that I got straight D's on my report card and that I had two detentions. A good week for me.

Aunt Joyce, like an indentured servant, filled everyone's water glasses and made sure the plate of mixed nuts was close enough for all of us to reach. Aunt Joyce was slender and stood straight up with perfect posture as if she went to finishing school. She wore a light-blue turtleneck sweater and khaki capris pants with her auburn hair puffed-up with hairspray.

"Harry is going to spend the night," Uncle Sy announced to everyone. "I want everyone to show him our finest hospitality," and he glared at both Joel and Eric.

"At 3 o'clock, I want Joel to take Harry and Eric to the high school field where you can toss the football around."

"Yes, Dad," Joel said as if he were addressing the Pope.

After lunch, we went to our rooms for our mandatory *quiet time*. I shared a room with Eric who put on his glasses and began to read a *Hardy Boys* book. I reached into my suitcase and pulled out a *Playboy*.

"What's that?" Eric asked in a squeaky voice.

"Oh, not much. Just a couple of really nice boobs on Miss July."

"Let me see! Let me see!" It was like a sick starving kid wanting to eat a pork chop for the first time. "If daddy ever finds out we'll be in trouble."

"Screw your daddy, Eric. He doesn't have to know what we're doing. I'm sure he has a whole closet full of this stuff."

I had another one in my duffle bag and tossed him an October. "Don't say I never gave you anything."

After quiet time, my cousins and I walked around their boring, ritzy neighborhood that didn't have any sidewalks and only a few traffic lights. We saw the big, rectangular synagogue with Moses and Aaron painted inside the glass windows where my cousins had their bar mitzvahs.

"Do you want to meet our rabbi?" asked Eric. "He's a really nice guy."

"Hell, no!" I told Eric. "I'm not going to set foot in one of those places again. The rabbi in my neighborhood almost sent me to prison just for playing basketball in his gym."

Uncle Sy's kids were raised corny and that's how they'll stay, playing everything by the book. They would never fit in where I lived. We didn't have parents who told us to go to synagogue every Saturday or who structured our time like a school teacher. We did everything for ourselves. If we wanted to play ball, we didn't wait for our parents to drive us someplace and organize it. We'd go to Max Meyers Playground with some baseball equipment, find an empty playing field, choose up sides, and have a game.

At the high school field, we tossed a football around. After a few long heaves, my arm got sore, and I wanted to do something with a little more excitement.

"This is boring shit," I told Eric and Joel. "Let's play a *real* game."

"Daddy said we should just to have a catch."

"Screw daddy!" I told Joel. "He's not here."

Joel waved to a couple of his friends who were headed back from a Scout meeting.

"Great," I said. "Now we could have a four on four."

I had never seen Uncle Sy's kids smile so much. They acted like a bunch of sad dweebs around their parents, always listening to them and never having any fun. But now, I could see them almost as being human.

As it turned out, they played like crap, but it was fun anyway. Joel called the plays like Curly of the Three Stooges rather than Bob Griese of the Dolphins. I lost because I had Eric on my team. He was slow, awkward, and couldn't catch even if you threw it underhand. He kept running in the wrong direction and fumbled before anyone touched him. After the game, we laid on the big sprawling lawn of the high school staring into the blue suburban sky.

I took out my pack of Marlboros and banged it on my fingers.

"Oh, you better put those cigarettes away before someone sees you."

"Don't worry, Joel, nobody's going to see me. There's no Gestapo around here."

Uncle Sy's kids looked at me in awe as I smoked the cigarette, obviously impressed that I knew how to smoke in the first place.

"Do you follow the Sixers?" I asked as the smoke rushed out of my nostrils.

"Sure," Eric said. "My Dad has season tickets."

Spoiled sonofabitch, I thought. Eric probably had front row seats and was able to eat all the hotdogs he wanted. I imagined my uncle driving his kids in his new air conditioned Cadillac with the seatbelts strapped tight while the rest of us patsies took the hot, crowded subway to South Philly.

It turned out that Eric didn't know squat about the Sixers. He couldn't come up with the starting lineup if his life depended on it, and he had no idea what position Fred Carter played.

"What position do you play, Eric?" I asked, hoping he knew that at least.

"Guard."

"Shooting guard or point?"

He shrugged his shoulders. Jeez, it was like talking to a sports imbecile. *Poor kid*, I thought. His control-freak father had destroyed his mind, making him ignorant of all the important things in life.

We made a slow trek back to the house as I finished another cigarette. Joel and Eric kept watching me smoke and flipping my stringy-brown hair from my eyes. It was as if they never saw a real person before.

Perhaps the best part of this crappy weekend was Uncle Sy's new 32-inch Sony Trinitron. The TV was connected to four speakers that filled up every corner of the living room.

"Oh great," I said, "basketball."

All of us sat on the sofa as we watched Billy Cunningham juke and jive out of the defenders' reach, piling up assists, and scoring off turnovers. You could almost touch him; the picture was that sharp and clear. For a moment, I forgot about being at Uncle Sy's house and enjoyed myself. I took the opportunity to explain what was going on in the game for my cousins. "That's a *give-and-go*" "That guy's *cherry-picking*." Joel and Eric seemed very impressed, learning something important for a change.

That didn't last long, however. At dinner, I was self-conscious again thanks to Uncle Sy asking me how my mother was and all I could say was that she was okay. The reality was that she was never okay. She was always in the midst of some emotional meltdown, and I never knew what mood she would be in next. Even if I told him the truth, he would complain and probably say something like: "See, I told your father that she needed to get psychiatric care sooner. He didn't listen to me. Now, look at her."

I was afraid that my cousins saw me as being unstable like my mother. And I also wondered if Uncle Sy viewed me as a pathetic charity case, and that the only reason he invited me to his house was that he felt sorry for me.

I ate everything on my plate. It was the best prime rib with mashed potatoes that I ever had. It was a lot better than the Chef Boyardee ravioli crap that my mother made in that old burnt saucepan of hers. Most of the time, I scrounged up a few dollars and went to Dante's Inferno for a pizza or a meatball grinder.

After dinner, we all took our plates and silverware to the sink and cleaned them. There were two sinks, one with clean water and the other full of detergent. I kept thinking of that damn magic word, *structure*, as I scraped the food off my plate, scrubbed it in the soapy water and then dipped it into the clean. Each of us dried off our plates with a separate dish towel and stacked everything back into the kitchen cabinet.

At 7 p.m., we played a game of Monopoly while Aunt Joyce sat in the corner of the room and read a romance novel. Uncle Sy quickly bought the Boardwalk and Park Place, but that was about it. Eric had a lot of cheap properties but didn't garner much rent. Joel had all the railroads and utilities and was pulling in the dough. I was stuck in jail half the time, passing Go only twice during the whole game. Everyone was pretty intense like their life depended on winning a lame game. I just enjoyed watching everyone stress out and seeing Uncle Sy go bankrupt.

It was way too quiet at night in Uncle Sy's house. You didn't hear any buses or trolleys. There were no loud police sirens or kids in their cars burning rubber. Just the sound of silence as if nothing else existed but you and the black, moonlit night. I'm sure Joel and Eric were used to this, but for me, it felt empty and barren, as if life had ended at 9 p.m. I lay awake wondering how people could sleep in such quiet. I looked out into the darkness, and all I could hear were the crickets and the leaves fluttering from some random tree.

Once the sun shone through the slats of the blinds the next morning, I knew it was Sunday. I got out of bed, packed my bag as quickly as I could and sat on the chair. I was ready to leave. I shared twenty-four hours with a family that made me feel like a second-class citizen. I wanted to go back to my life, back to the city where things were alive and spontaneous. I knew that when my uncle dropped me off at home, he would give me an envelope full of money that I would give to my mother to help with the rent. She would ask me how the weekend went, and I would say that it sucked and that I never want to go back. She would say, "If it weren't for your uncle, I wouldn't be able to afford to buy you those expensive sneakers you're wearing."

I heard Uncle Sy and Aunt Joyce's anxious chatter in the living room. Eric was putting on his good clothes. I looked out the window at my uncle's enormous yard with the six-foot-tall hedges that wrapped around his property like a noose around my neck. I dug into my pocket for a cigarette and opened the window.

Dark Clouds Over Baseball

All I had were my friends because I didn't have much of a family life. None of my friends ever saw my father play ball or have a catch with me, and whenever they saw my mother and me together, we were either arguing or she was chasing me around the block, throwing Coke bottles at me for no reason.

Sonny, one of my best friends, taught me how to play step ball in front of the house.

"If it goes past you, it's a single. If it's over your head, it's a double. A triple is when the ball hits a car and a homer is when it sails onto somebody's front lawn."

He always seemed to hit the step squarely on its edge, sending the pinkie ball over my head for a home run. He was a couple of years older and a lot bigger so he thought he knew everything.

Some days we'd gather all the kids we could find and go to the big grassy lot on Algon Avenue, put some cardboard bases down and play baseball. I was a singles hitter like Pete Rose. Sonny was a power pitcher like Sandy Koufax and Beetle thought he was the second-coming of Tim McCarver behind the plate. Sometimes I ran around the bases in my good Chuck Taylor's and would accidentally step in dog poop. I kept running, though, churning my little legs, trying to get to third base on a single and worry about the crap on my soles later.

On Sundays, when no one was around, I'd play by myself. I drew a big square on my garage door with white chalk for the strike zone. I imagined that I was Juan Marichal, swiveling my head in all directions and making a high leg kick as I delivered the sponge ball. I fantasized about pitching to Roberto Clemente and Hank Aaron, making them look silly with a wicked slider or a fastball up and in.

Beetle lived in a stone and brick row house with his mother a few doors down. He was called Beetle because he enjoyed popping open beetle shells and pulling their wings apart. His mother was from Germany and when she answered the door, I didn't understand a damn thing she said because of her thick German accent. It always smelled like mothballs and old musty clothing in his house.

He knew a lot of things that I didn't know and wasn't arrogant about it; that's why I liked him so much. He watched professional wrestling on his black and white RCA. His favorite wrestlers were Bruno Sammartino and Gorilla Monsoon because he said, "they were complete animals." He knew it was phony with fake blood and choreographed falls, but he thought it was the coolest thing ever.

Beetle also listened to 45s on his little GE record player. His favorite music was from the late fifties, especially the doo-wop groups like the Flamingos and the Platters who harmonized and wore snazzy tuxedos. It made him forget about his mother who dug her nails into his arms whenever he did something wrong. She dug so deep that it drew blood and left awful purple scabs that he picked at and immortalized like badges of honor.

I felt sorry for Beetle and had a sense that his life wouldn't turn out so well. I tried not to worry about him too much because I had my own problems. Even though my mother was crazy and my father rarely came home, at least they never punctured my arms with their nails.

When it rained and we couldn't play baseball, Beetle, Sonny and I would play a cool board game called *All Star Baseball*. It had a couple of spinning wheels and a bunch of discs that stood for each baseball player like Ruth, Foxx, and Williams. I desperately wanted the Ted Williams disc because he had the best chance of getting on base.

I kept pestering Sonny about the disc so much one time that he finally said, "Alright, asshole," and threw the Ted Williams disc at me with all his strength, but it veered off toward Beetle and almost hit him in the eye.

"What are you trying to do, blind me?" Beetle said.

Both Beetle and I stopped playing, leaving Sonny pissed and feeling that he screwed up a good game. We both felt that we took enough abuse in our families, and we weren't going to take any more from him.

My father bought my first *All Star Baseball* game in 1964. It was one of the happiest days in my life and one of the few times that my father did something nice for me, something that I *really* wanted. The game was wrapped tightly in cellophane and it had a brand new smell. It was so beautiful that I didn't want to open it at first. I stared at it for several minutes until I couldn't wait any longer and peeled the cellophane off with my fingernails.

"You're the best, Dad," I said when he brought home the game. But he was too tired to play with me that day, the next day, or any other day.

Dad lived upstate and owned a produce store on the highway. He came home when he felt like it, which wasn't too often, and he rarely let us know when he was coming. I'd be playing stepball or having a catch with my friends and I'd hear his truck's grinding gears coming around the corner. I would drop everything and run to him as fast as I could.

I once asked my Dad, "Why don't you live with us anymore?"

His glasses fogged up with tears, and he said, "Who would take care of the store?"

I nodded as if I understood. But I knew that the real reason was the he couldn't live with my *crazy* mother. It was bad enough that he had to see her once a month, but to live with her all the time would be too much. So, I never asked again.

I didn't ask him about his girlfriend, either. I figured that he had enough problems dealing with my mother, who also knew that he was seeing another woman. She never confronted him, but yelled and screamed whenever they got together, which would often embarrass me in front of my neighbors and friends.

"What's wrong with your parents?" Sonny asked. "I can hear them screaming way over the next block."

I shrugged my shoulders because I didn't know what to say. He was not the type of person to confide in. He wouldn't understand.

I loved Sonny, but I resented the fact that he had a good family. His father was always home and his parents never fought. Sonny looked like a baseball player and had the skills that could get him into the major leagues one day. I imagined him having a great life with a foxy-looking girlfriend and a lot of money.

I wasn't so sure about Beetle, though. He was more like me, perhaps destined not to be happy or have the things that Sonny would attain. I once saw a picture of Beetle's father who looked exactly like Humphrey Bogart. That's why Beetle was so good looking and lucky with the girls. Attractive girls always rang his doorbell to see if he was home. No matter where we went, there was always a cute girl flirting with him. He was so used to it that he didn't think there was anything special about it.

If you'd ask him, he'd say that he had high expectations. He wanted to go to a good college like Penn and study business, make a lot of money, and buy a sporting goods store when he got older. I always felt that he never really believed that he would make a lot of money or graduate from a prestigious college. Whenever he discussed his plans for the future, he seemed depressed like something would keep him from attaining his goals.

The day Beetle got hit in the head with a baseball there were dark, gray clouds in the sky.

We went to a grassy lot on Algon Avenue to play fungo. Sonny had a 34-ounce Louisville Slugger and a first baseman's glove. Beetle brought a few hardballs from home and a couple of gloves, including a brand new catcher's mitt.

The Orthodox Jewish kid, Shyman, had to borrow an extra glove from Beetle because his parents wouldn't let him play baseball, believing that Jews should study the Talmud all day and not waste time with secular kids like me. He said that he didn't care if his parents called him a "bad Jew," he was going to play baseball because he loved it more than anything.

Despite his enthusiasm for the game, we only let Shyman play when there was nobody else around because he was too uncoordinated and didn't know the subtleties of the game like the rest of us. This made him the perfect fungo player since he didn't have to know how to play; he just chased the baseball in the outfield and threw it back to the pitcher.

Shyman pinned a yarmulke to his hair and had a prayer shawl tucked under his clothing that made his behind lumpy. He had long, coiled side curls that bounced around his neck whenever he shagged a fly ball. He'd trip over his own two feet but always got up smiling, and gave it everything he had even when the dark clouds moved in and there was a light mist.

I finished tying the laces on my cleats and gripped the bat with both hands. I dug my heels into the dirt around home plate and held my bat cocked to the side like Pete Rose. I took a few practice swings while remembering to stay balanced at the plate.

Sonny made believe he was getting signs from Beetle, the catcher. He imagined he was checking the runner at first and then zinging in a 70 mph fastball that made a *pop* when it hit Beetle's catcher's mitt. I took a big swing and almost lifted off the ground, sending a fly ball deep into center field. Shyman lost his yamaka as he chased the fly ball that would eventually bounce in the street, and he was lucky enough to catch up to the ball before it went down the sewer.

I had always told Shyman not to play so shallow, that I'm a power hitter like Mays or McCovey and I could hit a fastball with my eyes closed. "That'll teach you a lesson!" I shouted. "You'll know better next time!"

While Beetle was in a catcher's squat, he turned to look at a foxy girl who had wandered onto the field not too far from home plate. She was a redhead with skinny long legs and ocean blue eyes, obviously attracted to Beetle by the way that she smiled at him.

Sonny wound up like his idol Sandy Koufax and threw an overhand fastball right by me and into the left temple of Beetle who, at the time, was looking at the girl instead of the pitcher. The baseball made a crunching sound when it hit his skull and knocked him backward into the backstop.

He lay sprawled on his back behind home plate, not moving, and no perceptible sign that he was still alive.

It reminded me of the time when I ran into a basketball stanchion in the schoolyard when I was in elementary school. I was chasing a mini-football and not looking where I was going. I had caught the damn football but I smacked my bony skull against the iron pole that supported the basket. All I saw were a bunch of spinning lights and felt a numb pain that went all through my body.

We thought for certain that Beetle was dead because his eyes were shut and we couldn't see his chest rising.

"Are you alright?!" shouted Sonny, looking as pale as a ghost.

Sonny shook Beetle's narrow shoulders and squeezed his mouth until his lips popped out. "Say somethin'!"

When Beetle finally opened his eyes, he was groggy for a few seconds, then a string of drool slid out of the corner of his mouth and just hung there. He had a bright red welt on the side of his forehead that seemed to grow with every passing moment.

We propped him up, opened a bag of Sugar Babies, and put some in his hand. Sonny wiped the saliva off Beetle's face and asked if he wanted to go to the hospital.

"No," Beetle shook his head, "let me sit first and stop my head from spinning."

He kept looking down at the brown dirt of the playing field, holding his Sugar Babies in one hand and feeling the throbbing lump with the other.

We surrounded him around home plate, collectively feeling traumatized and dazed, not knowing what to say or do. I picked up the ball and looked at the laces, trying to focus on something other than a friend moving in and out of consciousness. Sonny chewed on some Dubble Bubble, noticeably upset and guilty, no doubt blaming himself for this misery that took us all by surprise. Even Shyman looked disturbed, playing with his long side curls between his fingers.

The afternoon sky grew darker over our playing field. Soon we heard thunder rumbling in the distance.

We didn't play any more baseball that day. In fact, we didn't play a game for the rest of that summer.

Beetle sat on the grass next to the pretty girl who was looking at the huge lump on his forehead. Just as the rain came, the candy truck pulled up to the lot. We bought Candy Buttons, Milk Duds, and Sugar Straws hoping that candy was the elixir for all our troubles. We stood under a big oak tree eating our sweets and looking at poor Beetle clutching his head.

Sonny said how sorry he was and gave Beetle his box of Milk Duds. He was about to cry when Beetle consoled him.

"Don't worry, man. It was my fault. I should've been paying attention."

I was pretty certain that the hardball had something to do with Beetle killing himself ten years later. We stopped playing baseball that summer because Beetle kept going to doctor appointments and Sonny kept making excuses not to play whenever I knocked on his door. Pretty soon we outgrew each other, had different friends, travelled in different circles, and lost contact.

Years later, I found out through a mutual friend that Sonny dropped out of college and went from one lousy job to the next. He also told me that Beetle hung himself from a light fixture in his bedroom one day. His mother found him dangling from a rope tied to his neck. I'll bet she really felt guilty for digging her nails into his arms and treating him like his father.

When I first heard the news about Beetle, I thought about all the Rock Candy and boloney sandwiches we ate together while we listened to his doo-wop music or watched wrestling matches on TV. He was the first person who ever took a real interest in me and showed me what a condom looked like and how to smoke a cigarette. Even though he was older, he treated me like an equal.

It really pissed me off that Beetle never had a future as a business owner or that Sonny never made it to the big leagues. It bugged me that the collapse of their hopes and dreams was all due to a game that I loved, about a baseball that wasn't caught, that was thrown without any intention of hurting anyone or changing the trajectories of our lives.

Now that I'm grown, I know that these things happen for no rhyme or reason. Random acts occur in our lives that we don't expect or want. Just like it happened that my mother was crazy and my father rarely came home when I was a kid.

Regardless of what happened to Beetle and the problems I had growing up, I still look back on those summer days playing baseball with gratitude and not one ounce of regret. When I close my eyes, I remember the cool breeze coming through my window screen and the sweet smell of the city after a good rain shower. I'll always cherish those summer mornings when I woke up and realized that there was no school, hearing the sounds of rustling neighbors, birds chirping on the telephone lines, and lawnmowers cutting the green grass just right.

Sometimes, I dream of Sonny and Beetle standing in front of my old house in cut-off jeans and sneakers, chewing Dubble Bubble, and waiting for me to come outside and play a game of stepball or perhaps going down to the big lot on Algon Avenue to throw some baseballs around.

In my dreams, Beetle always catches the ball.

In my dreams, my parents were always together.

Weekend in Chelsea

I had been a loyal follower of Kevin for years. He was the kid with the nice curly hair, well-chiseled nose, straight teeth, and deep-set brown eyes. I, on the other hand, was average looking with hair that never laid right, tinsel teeth, and booger-green eyes. Kevin was the smart one, the strong one, and the person who called me every Saturday morning and told me what our plans were for the weekend. I was like his obedient dog, anticipating my master's call, never straying too far from the phone.

"You wanna go to Chelsea this weekend?"

"Sure," I said. "How much shall I bring?"

"At least fifty," he said. "We're going to stay overnight, find some cheap room somewhere."

"Cool."

I grabbed my bar mitzvah money from the drawer and took a few extra bucks from my mother's purse for good measure. I wore my best torn-off jean shorts, a pair of high-top Converse, and a Rolling Stones T-shirt that I'd bought at the Roosevelt Mall the weekend before.

Kevin rang the doorbell at 9:30 a.m. I stuck a note on the refrigerator for my mom, telling her where I was going and that I would call her once I got there. We walked to Levick Street and hitched a ride from a guy who had big, frizzy hair in a VW Bug with a bunch of antiwar stickers all over the back of his car. He was playing *Ticket to Ride* by the Beatles on an eight-track that we were all digging.

"Where are you dudes going?" he asked with a slur to his speech.

"A.C.," Kevin said.

"That's cool, but I'm turning off at Olga's Diner."

"No problem," we said, feeling the summer breeze coming through the open window and the grinding of the gears as we soon made it to Olga's.

It took us two more rides to get to Atlantic City, and by 2 p.m. we had finally made it to the boardwalk.

There was something about being down the shore that you couldn't find elsewhere. You became totally wrapped-up in the festive atmosphere. We took off our T-shirts and walked slowly along the boardwalk, breathing in the fresh air and eyeing the girls in string bikinis. The gigantic Ferris wheel kept turning and people screamed as the snaking roller coaster took them on a scary ride. We smelled the patchouli incense from the head shops and heard Jimi Hendrix playing "Crosstown Traffic." We got out of the way of men pushing the rolling chairs and had to move again when the tram car driver honked his horn and shouted "Move aside for the tram!" through the loud speakers.

We sampled nuts from the tray that Mr. Peanut held with his oversized hands. We watched the woman in the window make vanilla walnut fudge, tasted some chocolate marshmallow and decided to buy a huge chunk of it. We were warmed by the sun and felt relaxed by the sound of the ocean tide rolling in and out.

While eating a slice of greasy pizza and feeling proud of our shirtless bodies, two kids who were much older jumped off the railing and began chasing us until we ran toward a cop. We sat on a wooden bench for a while to catch our breath, feeling surprised that something bad could happen in Atlantic City.

We soon found a little room in an old Victorian house in Chelsea, just a few blocks from the boardwalk. The windows were wide open and had plenty of sunlight. There was a king size bed, two white rattan chairs on either side of the room, a couple of seashell ashtrays, a large oval mirror, and a freshly painted bureau with a lava lamp that didn't work.

Down the hall, Cream was playing on the radio. A girl was in the communal shower singing "Strange Brew."

A few minutes later, the singing babe came out of the shower wrapped in a towel with her hair wet and soap dripping down the side of her tan leg. She tiptoed into her room, but not before she turned to me and smiled. She left the door half-open and giggled with her girlfriend.

Kevin and I looked at each other in the most lascivious way without saying a word. For the next hour, we couldn't stop talking about the two girls down the hall. In our horny little minds, we were coming up with different scenarios on how we were going to get to know them and, hopefully, get in their pants.

"We could ask if there are any good places to eat and invite them out," I suggested.

"No, that won't work," Kevin scoffed, "we barely have enough money for the room."

"We could simply knock on their door and say, *Hi* and introduce ourselves."

Kevin was okay with that idea. He didn't like things to be too complicated. Without even asking, I knew that he would have the courage to initiate a conversation with the girls because I, frankly, didn't have enough confidence. I was too afraid that a girl would see a flaw in me and say something that was demeaning.

"It's a good idea, Harry, but I really think they dig older guys. Much older than us." So, it was a total surprise when we heard the girls' flip-flops squeaking toward our room. They knocked on our half-open door and asked if they could come in. They said that this was their last night and they wanted to have a little fun before they went back home.

My heart pumped all its blood to my face.

"You're too cute," the blonde told Kevin.

The girl with long auburn hair and bony knees smiled at me, despite my embarrassment.

"Can I sit on your bed?" the blond asked Kevin.

I've never seen Kevin so flustered. He was tongue-tied and all he could do was nod his head without uttering a word.

"Light My Fire" was playing down the hall as the blonde ran the tip of her forefinger over the bridge of Kevin's nose. "You're good looking, you know that?" she said. Kevin was still at a loss for words.

"Do you have a girlfriend?"

"Kind of."

The girls smiled at each other as if to say that they really got us. They knew that we were naive and took advantage of it. Kevin and I took turns blushing reds and purples, but we didn't mind one bit. Every moment that they were in this room felt like a lifetime of happiness, something that we'd only dreamed about.

"Do you mind if I smoke?" the auburn-haired girl asked me.

"Ah, no," I said reluctantly, knowing that it would affect my asthma and most likely make me wheeze for the rest of the night. But it was hard to refuse a hot girl with sexy bare legs stretched over your bed. When you're thirteen and as inexperienced as we were, you're open to almost anything.

I heard the sounds of the boardwalk arcade in my mind, the steel balls in the pinball machine bouncing off flippers and bumpers, the scoreboard lighting up something wild. I imagined playing the machine hard, rocking it just enough so the flipper could hit the ball without it going down the hole or making it tilt.

As the blonde fondled Kevin, the auburn-haired girl lured me to the opposite corner of the bed. She reached into her suede, frilly purse and pulled out a small Sucrets tin with several rolled joints inside. I watched the marijuana cigarette touch her light red lips ever so gently like all of this was going on in slow motion, watching her take one deep inhale after another until a foggy haze of reefer smoke covered us like a warm blanket.

"Your turn," she smiled. I paused, not knowing what to do as she carefully took the lit joint and placed it in my mouth like a kiss. My mind was telling me that it was alright, that it was medicine that I was sucking into my asthmatic lungs and not anything harmful. She could have convinced me to do almost anything and, as the cloud of smoke got thicker, she kept moving closer.

Kevin and the blonde made out with a fierce passion, smacking their lips with loud conviction. It inspired me to do the same with the beautiful girl by my side.

The auburn-haired girl propped herself against the headboard, spreading her legs and revealing a spectacular view. I became hard in an instant. But in all honesty, I didn't know what to do next. I wasn't Kevin. He knew what a woman wanted, probably from all the experience he had making out with his next-door neighbor, Sandra Cohen. He told me that he once had sex with her while listening to Emerson, Lake, and Palmer on the sofa before her mother came home.

My experience was just in my head, either thinking about the girls in my class or imagining what it would be like doing it with someone random. I hoped that the auburn-haired girl would literally take my hand and lead me in the right direction.

She pulled me closer and kissed my mouth as light as a feather. Her lips were so soft and hungry that they engulfed me. Her tongue found its way inside of my mouth as if it were a friendly serpent. She tasted like strawberry gum. I tried to keep my tongue inside of her as long as I could, but because I breathed through my mouth it was difficult to French kiss and to inhale air at the same time.

The next thing I knew she was removing my Rolling Stones T-shirt and massaging my chest with her warm hands, then slowly running her pink fingernails from my nipples to the edge of my pubes. Kevin was already naked at the other end of the bed and seemed to be intent on going all the way. The blonde was going down on him, her head undulating like a well-oiled machine as Kevin stared up at the ceiling like he was looking at the Sistine Chapel.

"Crimson and Clover" was playing on the radio.

It almost felt like a competition, a screw-off of sorts. The auburn-haired girl and I were going toe-to-toe while Kevin and his girl were doing the same. When I finally got head, it felt like the room was spinning and I was floating on the ceiling looking down at myself. Although I had a bar mitzvah last week, and the rabbi said that I was a man, it was only in that sexual instant did I feel manly. I couldn't imagine life getting any better.

I was in bed with a beautiful girl and not one of those imaginary ones I spent so much time alone with in my room. The auburn-haired chick slipped a condom on my penis with her mouth. Not only was she sexy but she was able to do really amazing things without any hands.

Once the condom was secure, the auburn-haired girl looked at me as if she were waiting for something special. Whereas, I was expecting guidance.

"Is this your first time?" she asked.

"Yes," I said, feeling weak and vulnerable right after *yes* came out of my mouth. There's nothing scarier than going against your ego, especially when it comes to telling the truth about sex. I expected her to laugh or give me a pathetic look but that's not how it happened. She gave me the most loving glance, as if to say *Oh, you're so sweet*.

"Well, get on top," she motioned with welcoming hands.

At the other end of the bed things were not going so well. The blonde got upset. She jumped off the bed and said that Kevin came too soon. She accused him of being an immature little schoolboy and said that she wanted a real man who knew how to please her. Kevin said something that he shouldn't have said and she snapped on her panties, turned to her girlfriend and shrieked, "Let's get out of here!"

For the first time in my life, I felt sorry for Kevin. He looked so devastated, totally humiliated at the hands of a beautiful but insensitive teenage girl. Rejection had never been something he had to deal with; everything seemed to come so easy for him. But now he was naked and rejected, vulnerable and embarrassed. His manhood in jeopardy.

Without saying another word, he sat up on the edge of the

bed, looked down at his bare feet, hoping to find an answer somewhere between his toes. After a while, he rose from the bed and shuffled to the bathroom like a man who had just lost his last penny in the stock market. He turned on the faucet and stood under the shower head, letting the hot, steamy water wash over his wounded ego.

For once in my life, I was the amazing one. I was the one with rugged good looks. The auburn-haired chick didn't want to leave me and told her friend to wait in her room because she's having fun. "Now, where were we?" she said and planted another kiss.

She placed my hand where she could feel the most pleasure and told me how soft or hard to touch her. She sighed and moaned in a way that made me feel honored and proud. When our passion slowly subsided, she said that I treated her with respect, better than most of the other boys that she had been with. She told me that her mom was picking her up in a little while and gave me a goodbye kiss on the cheek. She wrote down her phone number on my hand in blue ink with *love* and *kisses*.

"I really want to hear from you," she said. The moment those words came out of her mouth, I knew I would never see her again. Not because I didn't want to, but because I wanted to keep that moment sacred. In my mind, she had made a lasting impression, a beautiful sexual angel who came into my life for a brief moment to give me a precious gift of self-confidence and then gracefully float away.

It was shortly after my first sexual encounter that I realized that I have always underestimated myself. I was a lot more competent than I gave myself credit for. I was on par with Kevin in every way but I never saw it, had convinced myself that I was a marginal person and that I would never be popular. That weekend in Chelsea opened my eyes to what I could be. I may not have thick curly hair, a well-chiseled nose, or sexy brown eyes but I had something that many teenagers my age didn't have.

I had a belief in myself.

The auburn-haired girl taught me that all I had to do was be honest and vulnerable and people would respond favorably. If I told the truth, I would get more of what I wanted.

As for Kevin, we never talked much about what happened to him during our weekend in Chelsea. He acted like that weekend never existed, but he couldn't hide the fact that he was a changed kid once he got back to Philly. He didn't have the same amount of confidence. He became humble, more willing to let me plan our weekends and, most incredibly, initiate conversation with girls. He finally realized who his best friend really was, a very cool guy.

The Psychedelic Basement

Shawn and I were walking to school Friday morning like any normal day. Shawn was wearing bell bottoms with moccasins and a loose fitting white button-down collar shirt. I wore dark Levi jeans with chukka boots and a tan V-neck sweater over a white undershirt.

"Dude," Shawn said, "do you want to cut school?"

He always referred to me as *dude*.

"Why don't you come over my house and we can chill?" he said.

He didn't have to coax me very much.

"I fixed up my basement, dude. I want you to tell me what you think."

"Cool," I replied, not worrying about whether my mother would find out. My father always said, "What they don't know won't hurt them." I gave my mother no indication that I smoked pot or took off from school on occasion. It was our last year of high school and my friends and I felt entitled to skip a day or two.

We walked to his brick split-level on Friendship Street. He had the keys to his backdoor and we strolled past the Maytag washer and dryer in the hallway until we came to his basement.

He switched on the light and the world of rock music seemed to crystalize right before my eyes.

"This is so cool!" I said as my jaw dropped.

Shawn had painted his entire basement black, including the ceiling. He put a strobe switch under the light bulb and the light seemed to flicker to the beat of the music and made his Jimi Hendrix and Moody Blues posters have a phosphorescent glow. The rock stars on the wall were 3-D and literally came alive.

"My mom is working late," Shawn said. "Fishman might stop by later."

Fishman was our friend from our high school fraternity, Zeta Rho. He had a pizza delivery job on Castor Avenue as part of a work study program at school. He used to play football for Northwest but got kicked off the team for coming to practice stoned on numerous occasions.

I took a seat on the sofa while Shawn placed the vinyl on the turntable, "Nights in White Satin," one of my favorite songs.

It was a song that I understood intuitively but I didn't have the words to explain. Every time I heard it, I felt I was being carried away to a distant place where time froze and where stoners got laid by sexy goddesses born out of the pages of *Playboy*.

Shawn had a different interpretation. He thought of a girl named Cindy Waller, a stereotypical flower-child with long strawberry-blonde hair who often sunbathed on the big sprawling lawn in front of our high school. Shawn had the hots for her but she never gave him the time of day. He sent her notes in English class, stuck letters in her locker, and got her friends to put in a good word for him but she just ignored Shawn. She was an aloof butterfly who looked like Goldie Hawn.

"Unrequited love," Shawn said, "that's what that song is about."

I didn't really care what the song was about. All I knew was that it made me feel like I was floating in the upper stratosphere of who knows where.

Shawn lit a stick of incense that smelled like a cacophony of animal and garden aromas.

"You don't mind, do you?" Shawn asked, "I've been meaning to try this shit forever but I never got the opportunity."

The incense smelled like I was inside of a head shop on South Street. It had a funky odor that you could probably smell at a Cream concert.

"It's patchouli," Shawn said.

I didn't know patchouli from *blazing hemp* or any of the other kinds of incense they sold on South Street. I just knew that it brought up memories, feelings, images of tie-dye shirts, and the smell of a frilly suede jacket worn by Roger Daltrey of The Who.

As the strobe light flickered, another song blasted from Shawn's thirty-inch speakers, the best stereo system I've ever heard with an amazing pair of woofers and tweeters. It made the Grateful Dead's "Friend of a Devil" seem like it was playing right here in the basement with Jerry Garcia and Bob Weir.

The Dead reminded me of the summer when Shawn and I were down the shore in Atlantic City. There was a strung-out guy who jumped out a restaurant front window, apparently tripping on LSD or magic mushrooms. He came through a pane of glass and ended up in the middle of Baltic Avenue with his skin shredded, blood pouring out, and then he decided to lay down in the middle of a busy intersection, stopping traffic.

When the cops arrived, the guy gets up and starts to run away and does a figure-eight while they're chasing him. You really can't outrun the cops when your mind is exploding on mushrooms or when blood is gushing out of you like a geyser.

"I sure feel like a joint right now," Shawn said, laying on the other couch with his hands running through his shoulder-length black hair.

"Me three," I said, meaning *too*.

I really didn't care if I had a joint or not. Being in Shawn's basement was the most relaxing thing I could think of doing besides floating in a pool of water. And pot doesn't always make an experience better because of the paranoid factor. Whenever I got high, I kept thinking that the cops were going to bust in on us or that my parents would find out.

"Down by the River" by Neil Young finished playing and Shawn quickly put a new record on the turntable. He had great taste in music and he always let you know about it.

"I bet you never heard of this band," he said proudly, and played a cut from New Riders of the Purple Sage.

He had an older brother named Mason who went to Penn that probably turned him on to new sounds even though Shawn said that he discovered the music by himself.

Time seemed to pass quickly without us knowing it. It was already four o'clock and we were still slumped over the sofa listening to jamming guitars and thinking about random stuff that would make little sense to anyone else.

"People are Strange" by the Doors made me think of my father who lived in Hazleton. After school lets out for the summer, I usually spent a couple of months working at his produce store, hanging out with the kids I've known from the summers before. I'd ride my Yamaha dirt bike in the splintered sunlight of the woods and race up and down the winding country roads of Cunningham Valley.

I looked at Shawn on the couch across from me. He was gazing at the strobe light and running his fingers through his hair. His dad left him when he was six. He didn't like to talk about his father, referring to him as an *asshole supreme*. The way his mom told the story, his dad ran off with a woman from Jersey. They're shacking-up somewhere in Oregon now, and he didn't even tell Shawn he was leaving, just sent a postcard a few months later saying that he's okay and that he's enjoying life again.

My father at least had the decency to tell me in person that he was leaving. He and I had a man-to-man talk on the front steps of our duplex. "It's the best thing for you," he said, "since your mother and I are always fighting. It's not good for children to be in the middle of that."

I remember crying for the longest time, feeling that the tears would never dry up. I was very angry at him at first, but after I had some time to digest it, I realized that my life was a lot better without my parents together.

There was a knock and rattle at the basement screen door. At first, I thought I was just being paranoid about the cops again.

The patchouli incense, coupled with the psychedelic basement, made me dizzy with fear.

"Oh, shit. It's only Fishman," I sighed when I saw his big body walk into the dark basement.

Fishman came in wearing a baggy pair of white carpenter pants and an old Northwest High football jersey with a pizza box in his right hand. He always wore a shitty grin like he was up to no good.

Of course, he was stoned, yelling about some customer who was an idiot. In the box, he had a whole New York cheesecake that he swiped from the refrigerator at work. I liked Fishman for the most part. He was good if you needed someone to fight a bully at school or as a defensive lineman when we played football on the Algon lot.

Give him an audience and you could bet that Fishman would start trouble, like that day we visited a fraternity house in Delaware. He had too much vodka to drink. All of a sudden, he's tearing up the joint, bouncing off furniture, knocking things over, breaking pictures—totally out of control. So, whenever I'm around him, I get anxious, worrying that he'll do something crazy.

"I got three mega joints in my pocket," he said proudly. "Hoberman turned me on."

Hoberman was his co-worker at the pizza joint. He was also a pot dealer on the side.

Shawn took the first drag and then passed it around. Every time I looked at the strobe light, the room spun like one of those rides at the amusement park where you lean against the wall and spin around so fast that the floor drops from under you.

Fishman wouldn't stop talking. Some people talk a lot when they're high, but I just laugh. I laugh not knowing what I'm laughing about because everything seems funny in the moment. Even the cheesecake in the pizza box staring at me on the floor seemed hilarious.

I grabbed a big slice of cheesecake and held onto it with all my fingers and didn't use a fork or a plate. I laid on the sofa, taking a bite and then resting the cheesecake on my chest, taking a drag of grass, laughing hysterically, and handing the joint back to Shawn. I don't remember how many slices of cheesecake I ate but I know that after a while it became really dry in my mouth and hard to swallow. I was too stoned to get off the couch and get a glass of water to wash it down.

Then Fishman said something funny and I couldn't stop laughing. Without thinking, I stuffed a big piece of cheesecake into my mouth and couldn't get it down. It was stuck there like a nail in a piece of wood. I couldn't spit it out or dislodge it no matter how hard I tried to swallow or cough.

Shawn was blowing big puffs of smoke and watching them as they made their way up to the black ceiling.

Fishman was oblivious to my struggle with the cheesecake. He jumped on the sofa like it was a trampoline, annoying the hell out of Shawn.

"Dude, stop it!" Shawn kept yelling to no avail. At this point, Fishman was going psycho. He was high, aggressive, and thought he could do anything and get away with it.

I couldn't get any air into my lungs. I took short, raspy inhales. Now the cheesecake was really stuck in my throat.

"Are you all right, dude?" Shawn asked, seeing that I was in distress while trying to get Fishman to stop jumping on the couch.

Shawn got pissed and tried to pull Fishman by the legs off the sofa, but he was too big. Fishman kicked Shawn in the head and threw punches that missed the target as the marijuana smoke filled the basement.

By then I had panicked, got up from the sofa, thinking that if I stayed there any longer, I would have suffocated.

I felt like a cat with a super hairball stuck in my throat as I made my way to the back door.

Once outside, I coughed up a chunk of cheesecake and was able to partially inhale some fresh air. I looked up at the late afternoon sun and felt grateful. I told myself to breathe through my nose so I could calm down. After a few more hard gulps,

I was able to swallow the rest of the cheesecake and resume normal breathing. Exhausted, I sat down under an elm tree in Shawn's backyard and watched my hands shake.

I could have died in my friend's basement that day. What's worse, I could have been lying dead by the basement door and my two friends would have still been fighting or passing around a joint with no inclination to check on me.

In time, Shawn would most likely come outside and find a slab of cold rigor mortis by the door, probably after he finished off another slice of cheesecake. "Holy crap! Mitchell is dead," he'd cry. "My mother will go ballistic!"

Fishman would most likely be still ramped up, making some sick joke about my demise and ignore my corpse completely, then go back inside for the rest of the cheesecake. "There's nothing we can do about it, dude," he'd say. "He's totally wasted."

I didn't bother to go back into the basement and tell my friends that I was alright. My look into the future pissed me off so much that the pure sight of them would have made my stomach turn.

I walked slowly home, touching my sore throat as I went along, still feeling a residual high and hearing the lyrics of "Nights in White Satin" play in my head. I think I figured out what the song meant on my way home but I soon forgot it once I snuck past my mother who was watching *The Match Game* on TV.

I collapsed on my twin bed, passed out, and slept like a baby for the rest of the evening.

My mother never suspected a thing.

Santiago on Percussion

I was downstairs at the Jambone with a guy who had an oddly-shaped head, swollen cheeks, and a speech impediment that reminded me of Elmer Fudd. He asked me to play chess. Since I felt anxious about being there and nothing to do with my hands, I agreed.

"What's your name?" I asked and shook his hand.

"Maylwin."

"Is that with a 'y' or without?" I asked.

"Wid out."

So, I called him Malwin without the 'y' since Maylwin would be way too difficult to pronounce.

We soon engaged in a game of chess. We were the only two people down in the semi-finished basement of the Jambone where they kept their coffee supplies and a staff restroom.

People upstairs were talking in a loud chatter and were walking on the creaky wooden floors to get to their seats. My ex-band was setting up right above my head. I could hear Glenn strumming his acoustic guitar, Brian plucking the strings of his bass, and Rosie taking short, choppy blows on the flute.

Our acoustic group was called the Blue Cradle—two guitarists, a flute player and me, a percussionist. Glenn originally named the band White Candle, but someone in town already had that name, and Blue Cradle sounded more mystical.

I felt like a folk music pariah, sitting on a wobbly wooden chair with Malwin, the guy with the odd-looking face but playing a mean game of chess. Even though his body was out of kilter, it did not affect his chess skills. He captured my most important pieces in less than ten minutes, and all I had left were a few pawns and a queen. It was just a matter of time until my queen was gone as well.

"My stage name is Santiago," I told Malwin. "My real name is Eddie."

He nodded and then moved his rook strategically across the board with the confidence of a Bobby Fisher.

"Glenn thought that my real name was too bland," I told Malwin. "That's why he dubbed me Santiago and told me to wear round shades like Carlos Santana."

I could hear the feedback from the microphones upstairs and guitars being tuned. Rosie was doing a popular riff on her new wooden flute that she bought from a Native American when she was vacationing in New Mexico.

"Yah moob," said Malwin.

"I learned the bongos watching PBS," I told him. "There's a guy from Trinidad who looks just like Bob Marley and plays the funkiest African-Caribbean rhythms."

Malwin's chess pieces surrounded me. I'd lose no matter where I moved. Chess wasn't my top priority at the moment. My band was warming up and soon they would play 'Part of the Plan" by Dan Fogelberg. I loved that song. I could play it with my eyes closed.

I knew I shouldn't be here. I had an Eastern Philosophy exam the next day and I still didn't understand the principles of Shintoism. My GPA was barely passable so I needed to bone up on my studies before the end of the quarter.

But it was the band that I kept thinking about, and those smoky rehearsals that drove a wedge between me and my bandmates.

They liked smoking pot more than rehearsing our songs. Pretty soon our rehearsals turned into a laugh fest and I was the only one not laughing. I sat there with the bongos between my knees waiting for the black, purple haze of marijuana smoke to lift so my eyes could stop burning.

But the smoke never lifted. It surrounded us like a toxic cloud.

I confided in Malwin even if he didn't really care or, perhaps, didn't understand. I told him that the band couldn't play without smoking dope. They didn't care if they weren't making progress with their music or not practicing enough. They thought I was a loser for not partying with them.

"Could you believe that they thought that I was the loser?"

Malwin didn't answer. He studied the chess pieces with his lower lip dangling off his face.

"Rosie was the only person in the group who had sympathy for me," I said. "She never called me a loser or put me down."

Malwin briefly looked up from the chessboard to pick his nose.

"I began to miss some rehearsals, thinking that they wouldn't notice and then I got a message that something was wrong. Glenn eventually realized that I was gone, and gave me a call."

"Yah moob," Malwin said.

"Glenn didn't want to hear what I had to say. He called me a slacker and told me if I didn't want to do the rehearsals then I would be out of the band."

I didn't tell Malwin that Brian called me a headcase, but I did tell him that Brian believed that smoking marijuana was an important part of making music. "If we took the grass out of music, it wouldn't sound as good."

I think Malwin muttered "bullshit" under his breath but I wasn't sure.

"I want to be upstairs playing my bongos with the band, Malwin, but I have to take care of myself. There are more important things in life. Don't you think?"

Malwin nodded his head in agreement. He pointed to the brown and white chessboard indicating that I should focus on the game and stop talking.

I lost my queen because I didn't see his knight lurking behind a row of pawns. Malwin grinned like a Cheshire cat, swooped in for the queen and cradled it in his stubby fingers for a few moments before setting it down with the other captured pieces.

"It was foolish of me to hope that the band would want me back, even though Glenn saw me earlier and appeared to give a friendly glance. From what I hear, they were planning to bring in a conga player from West Philly for a tryout."

Malwin put me in check by surrounding me with his bishop and queen. The only thing I could do was retreat.

"Ah-nudder?" he asked.

"The game's not over yet, take it easy," I said.

But in a few short minutes and four moves, there was no place for my king to go. I was trapped.

"Checkmate!"

Malwin's eyes lit up like two burning candles. He shook in the chair with glee for a few seconds, and blew his nose into a red hanky.

"Ah-nudder?" he asked again.

I shook my head no. "It would be too painful to be downstairs while my band was playing without me," I said.

I gave Malwin a handshake and complemented him on his masterful chess techniques and his undeterred concentration, strapped the gym bag containing the bongos over my shoulder, and headed for the back door.

I planned to take the long way back to Hilliard Dorms, past the oak trees on College Avenue. Those big, loping trees and the wide walkway always relaxed me and helped with any emotional turmoil.

"Santiago!" a voice crackled from the microphone system upstairs. I took my hand off the doorknob, turned my head. Did I hear that right?

"Will Santiago please come to the stage!"

It was Glenn's voice. And he repeated, this time even louder: "Attention! Will Santiago please come to the stage!"

"Holy crap!" I muttered in surprise, unless there's another Santiago, my guys were calling for me. They really wanted me back!

I stopped for a moment to decide what I was going to do. Should I play or should I go back to the dorm and study for the Eastern Philosophy exam? I briefly weighed the pros and cons in my head, but it was a no-brainer.

I looked at Malwin, who seemed to be playing chess by himself, "That's me they're calling for, dude. That's my band!"

"Ah-nudder?" he asked again, hoping for a different answer.

"No way, Malwin! My percussion skills are needed."

"Bedder tay car ah yer selv," Malwin muttered.

I shook my head, "I will. Thanks for reminding me, buddy."

I took a pair of dark blue Ray-Bans out of my shirt pocket and slipped them on. I rolled up my flannel shirt and removed the red marble bongos from the gym bag and quickly tightened up the heads with a silver key to get them tuned right.

I raced up the stairs like a wild man, tripping on the top step and knocking into a table where a couple sat, accidentally spilling their coffee.

"Hey man, watch it!" the guy yelled.

"I'm Santiago," I said proudly. "That's me they're calling for."

They didn't share my enthusiasm, but it didn't matter. I was headed to the stage again. The place where I felt most at home.

I weaved in and out of the tables, making sure I didn't spill any more coffee. It was hard seeing with my Ray-Bans but I had to maintain my image.

I finally made it to the stage, unscathed and out of breath.

Glenn announced to the crowd: "Here's our percussionist, the one and only Santiago Espanada!"

It was a pretty decent audience response with mixed clapping and hooting.

I was surprised that Glenn gave me a different last name without consulting me first. Although Espanada did sound a lot better than Meyers.

I took my rightful place on stage. I sat to the left of Glenn and Brian and alongside of Rosie. The guys gave me a thumbs-up sign and Rosie gave me a kiss on the cheek.

I was hyped and ready to go, gently massaging the steer-skin heads of my bongos with my fingertips like I do every time I'm about to play. I hadn't practiced for a few days but once I had those skins wedged between my knees, I relaxed and my natural instincts took over.

The lights in the coffee house went dim except for the overhead spotlight on the stage.

Glenn stomped his black leather boot on the wooden floor and quickly began the set, "a one, a two…"

The chords were stuck, the bass was plucked, and Rosie's flute sounded more beautiful than it's ever been as we moved into our first number, "Part of the Plan."

I never skipped a beat. The bongos comfortably resting between my knees—the small drum to the left and the large to the right—I played like I had done so many times before in college.

I knew that my joy would be temporary, however, that the marijuana haze would never disappear from our rehearsals. I realized that the band members would never stop being stoners. It was a part of who they were, part of their youthful identity. But on this night, on this stage at the Jambone with a packed house, I was Santiago Espanada on percussion playing a crazy African-Caribbean beat, even if it was the last set that I would ever play with them.

Mrs. Lindy's Boarding House

"Don't leave dishes in the sink or we'll have ants," Mrs. Lindy said. "If we ever do, just sprinkle some salt on them—that'll kill 'em."

I shook my head, visualizing an army of ants carrying forks and spoons on their backs, taking over the kitchen.

"We share the refrigerator," she said while opening the door of the old Frigidaire. "This section is yours, that's mine, and Mahsa has the middle shelf. Don't keep the freezer door open or you'll run up the electricity bill."

I nodded and promised I wouldn't keep the refrigerator door open too long.

"You seem like a nice person," she smiled, revealing her yellow teeth. "If you're noisy, or use drugs—you're out! Got that?"

I told Mrs. Lindy that I just drink herbal tea and that I have one close friend whose only vice is writing bad poetry.

We walked up the creaky steps to the bedrooms. My room was spacious with plenty of windows overlooking a large oak tree. Sunlight shone through the vertical blinds. The room consisted of a mattress and box spring, an unpainted bureau, and a rattan chair underneath a picture of an Italian countryside.

Mahsa had the other room at the far end of the hallway. She was a sophomore at Temple and, according to Mrs. Lindy, was very quiet. "She spends most of the day at school, comes home late and goes straight to her room."

"Sounds like a dedicated student."

"Try not to hog the bathroom," Mrs. Lindy swiftly changed the subject. "We do our business, clean up, and get right out. No dilly-dallying!"

I agreed to the terms and put down a security deposit. My expectation was simple. I would have a quiet room where I could write and have a kitchen to make simple meals. The TV in the living room was old but was adequate to watch the 6 o'clock news.

The first couple of months went according to plan. I drove to the Regional Library the same time every morning, researching my stories, and using the library computer. I wrote all my fiction longhand, going through three or four marble composition books every week. I returned home, watched the news on TV, ate a sandwich, and then read a novel for the rest of the evening. It had been a dream come true since I received a small inheritance from my Uncle Leo.

The more time I spent in the library, the better my stories got. Every day flowed seamlessly into the next, giving me a sense of focus and continuity without any obstacles or attachments to get in the way of my work.

After a particularly productive day, I was drinking a cup of hot tea and watching the news, when the phone rang. I assumed that it was my friend Bryan, who usually called to ask if I could meet him at Dunkin' Donuts to hear a couple of his new poems.

Instead, it was a crying female on the other end.

"Who is this?" I asked.

"It's Mahsa," she said through her cries. "It's awful! I'm in so much pain!"

I didn't know what to say.

"They pulled a tooth," she mumbled.

"Pulled a tooth?" I repeated.

"Yes, I didn't know who to call."

"Where are you?" I asked. "Do you want me to pick you up?"

"I'm at the Temple Dental School," she mumbled through her cheek stuffed with cotton gauze. "I'm okay. I just needed to talk to someone. I feel so alone."

"I'll drive there and get you," I offered.

"No, please don't. It's not your problem."

When she calmed down, she told me that she had two wisdom teeth pulled. She blamed herself for eating too many sweets and not having good dental hygiene. She kept saying that she did it to herself.

"Don't blame yourself," I consoled. "It happens to everyone."

"You *don't* understand; I never eat sweets. I only started to eat cake and candy when I moved to America."

Mahsa came home on the East Bound subway and the 66 bus. She slowly climbed the stairs to her bedroom and, in the silence of the evening, I could hear her faint cries and whimpering. I wanted to comfort her, to dry her tears, to be of some help, but I didn't know her well enough.

The next morning Mahsa knocked on my door. I had only seen her in passing, but now she stood in plain sight. She had a kind, oval face, dark and exotic features, and her long thick hair hung softly on her shoulders.

"Thank you for putting up with my childish behavior," she said, being careful not to smile with her sore gums.

Her brown eyes took my breath away.

"Don't worry, Mahsa. We all have our moments."

She sat on the rattan chair under the tacky Italian landscape. She felt homesick for her family in Iran. Her father was a banker, her mother a housewife, and she had two younger sisters and an older brother that she sorely missed. "My father is a wonderful man," she said and showed me a picture of him standing in front of the bank where he worked. "He believes in my dream of designing modern homes in Iran and paid for me to attend school in the States."

What she told me was not so unusual, but the way she looked and the softness of her voice was compelling.

"What does your name mean?" I asked.

"Like the moon," she said. "When I was born, my mother looked in my eyes and saw the moon's reflection."

The moon, I thought. *She's as perfect as the moon.*

* * *

Two weeks later, we were caught in the park during a rainstorm. I covered Mahsa's shivering body with my arms as we slowly made our way down the grassy hill. I watched the rainwater drip off the strands of her dark curls and tasted her sweet and salty mouth.

She bit my upper lip as the thunder and lightning rocked the nighttime sky.

As if a bolt of lightning hit us, we fell to our knees on the grassy knoll where she let me take off her blouse and unsnap her bra. I kissed her hard, perky nipples and ran my tongue down the creases of her body. We were oblivious to the cold, the rain splashing, and the muddy puddles forming around us.

"We better head back," she said reluctantly.

We held each other as we walked down the rain-soaked street under the blurry streetlights and dangling telephone lines. We finally made it to our front door and up the stairs to Mahsa's bedroom. Mrs. Lindy was out of town, visiting her grandchildren for the weekend.

"I've never done it before," she whispered.

I felt her warm breath on my chest.

"Whatever you want," I said. "I'm not rushing you."

I brushed the hair from her eyes.

She wanted to have me inside of her, but she was afraid of betraying her family. She feared becoming an outcast from the culture that she loved. Having sex before marriage, particularly with a Jewish man, was taboo. Her parents would disown her.

She stopped kissing me and looked out the rain-soaked window.

In my heart, I knew I was the wrong person for her, not a part of her dream or her future plans, but I couldn't let go.

She turned to me, then closed her eyes, not wanting to see what she was about to do. She unfastened my belt and reached into my pants. Her fingers trembled, cold with fear. She cried and said that she couldn't do it.

"It's okay," I said.

She grew silent and moved away from me. It felt as though there were continents separating us even though it was only the width of the bed.

The next day, I was in the kitchen talking with Mrs. Lindy as she was cranking open a can of chicken. She warned me about falling in love with Mahsa.

"I'm not blind, you know. Mahsa's a beautiful girl. I see the way the two of you look at each other and whisper things behind my back. Don't get carried away or you'll regret it."

I didn't tell Mrs. Lindy that I loved Mahsa and that she was all that I thought about. I promised Mrs. Lindy that I wouldn't break any rules in the house or cause any trouble.

"We're strictly friends," I lied.

"I hope so. You two are from opposite sides of the world."

Mrs. Lindy's eyes were tearing as she peeled an onion. "I'm telling you from past experience. Don't get stuck on a woman who isn't right for you. Your cultures are too different. You'll never be happy if you marry Mahsa."

She added mayonnaise to the chicken salad and probably was remembering a time that she fell in love with someone who let her down. She must have been hurt bad because her eyes were tearing even when she stopped peeling the onion.

Mahsa and I were out driving one night in my sky blue Karmann Ghia, when she asked, "Can I drive?"

She moved beside me despite the car having bucket seats, nudging the back of her head against my chin while her slender brown hands clutched the narrow steering wheel. It didn't matter if she had no clue how to work a stick shift or that she veered too close to parked cars, I could never say *no* to Mahsa.

"Do you like me?" she asked.

"Yes, of course."

"How much?"
"More than anything," I said, extending my hands far apart.
"Well, you shouldn't. You shouldn't like me so much."
"Why not?"
"Because you'll get hurt."

She looked up from the steering wheel, and a tear fell from her eye. I followed that tear down her face until it dropped from her chin.

At that moment, I didn't realize what was happening. Only the next day did I understand what she meant. When I was at the library working on a story, she moved to another part of the city trying to forget I ever existed. I found a letter on my bedroom floor. She apologized for leaving so abruptly and not saying goodbye, but she was sure that it was the best move. She said she wasn't right for me and that I should marry someone of my culture. She wrote a few other things that I skimmed over and she ended the letter with, "I'll always remember that night in the rain."

There was no return address or phone number, just the scent of her hair lingering in my mind and the empty room down the hallway where I once laid on her bed gazing into her brown eyes.

Dreams lasted longer, I said to myself standing in the middle of the room. I don't know how long I stood there with the letter in my hand.

In the next few months, I went to Mahsa's school and hung around the campus expecting to see her walk out of class, foolishly believing that if she saw me, she would change her mind. I kept reading her letter trying to find a word or phrase that told me that things weren't over, while knowing in my heart that it wasn't healthy for me to obsess over her.

I began to spend more time in the library than usual, and more time leafing through novels that spoke about unrequited love, trying to find an answer somewhere in the pages of the classic writers. But I didn't find any words of hope from Ernest Hemmingway or Somerset Maugham, just more sadness and disappointment.

It was painful letting go of Mahsa, but in time it got easier.

I stayed two more years at Mrs. Lindy's Boarding House. Eventually, the money ran out, and I had to get a real job. I gave up writing for a while. I became a psychologist and met an Israeli grad student who very much resembled Mahsa. We married after graduation, settled down in a trendy Philadelphia suburb, and had two children.

Sometimes, I look up at the sky when there is a full moon and see Mahsa's eyes staring down at me and remember the few moments we spent together as if it were a dream. I wonder now, as I did then, if the sweetness of the moonlight would ever change.

Room Full of Strangers

My father's girlfriend, Rosalie Chalinski, greeted me in the crowded living room, a room that looked more like a Christian clubhouse than a warm, comfortable place to say my last goodbyes to a father that I had once loved.

"Mike, your father's in the family room. He's been in a coma for several days."

My father was once a very strong man, able to lift hundred pound bags of potatoes with ease. He had Popeye forearms and a big, round Mr. Clean bald head. That day in the family room I saw him as a shriveled-up bag of bones.

I tried to feel sympathy and remorse, but all I felt that day was the annoying presence of strangers in a room where my dying father lay unconscious.

It was hard for me not to feel anger for him. He was a lifelong womanizer, a lover of pornography, and a frequent customer of the local houses of prostitution.

But I tried my best to see him as that little boy who had green eyes and a head full of blondish hair. He made money hawking Hershey bars on a Pottsville street corner. He moved to Philly after his mother's divorce and worked at her neighborhood luncheonette on Girard Avenue making soda from seltzer and flavored syrup. One day he dropped his white apron, quit high school, and went to work at a lighting factory in Bristol with his best friend. He got his GED and went to night school at Temple University to become a draftsman. But after a few years of working for someone, he became dissatisfied and went back to his family's produce business.

When I looked at Morton Lapides gasping for air, I saw images of a person's life that I knew as a child from a photo album. Before he met my mother, he wore a woolen Army uniform and served in the Korean War as a quartermaster. He doled out Army supplies, and spent much of his free time with Italian prostitutes that he paid in bars of soap. He also took his Kodak camera and shot pictures of the Eiffel tower, the Leaning Tower of Pisa, and the hundreds of crosses in fields of the Normandy American Cemetery. He was a man with an artistic inclination, but he chose the more practical route when he decided to marry my mother, Lilly. She was a beautiful woman who some said resembled Elizabeth Taylor but with a few screws loose. Grandma noticed this right away and warned my father not to marry her, but Mort was too far down the marriage path to turn back.

The strangers in the room loved Mort because he gave them free red delicious apples and topped off their strawberry baskets. Because someone gives you free fruit doesn't mean you should idolize him like the Pope. And that's what everyone in the room did. Their love for Mort made me sick to my stomach.

I detached from the strangers by watching TV, staring at happy people eating greasy McDonald's hamburgers, and then unhappy people taking Prilosec for acid indigestion. My stomach churned and growled with each commercial. I asked Rosalie for a Prilosec or a Zantac, but before she could get one from the medicine cabinet, I barfed all over her floral-patterned couch. I hadn't puked since third grade. That was the time I ate too many chili-dogs at Coney Island.

As Rosalie wiped off my vomit-soaked cheeks, I gazed at my father's sweaty, pale face with his frogmouth taking short, bubbly breaths. With each exhale there was a pop, like a cork bursting from a champagne bottle. *Why isn't he dead yet?* I wondered. *What's keeping him going?*

Just a few months ago, Mort was waking up at three in the

morning, putting on his work clothes, and traveling to South Philly to buy fruits and vegetables. The Food Center was an open-air market inhabited by crude oddballs who used the f-word like golfers used woods and irons. My father fit into this foul-mouthed environment because he was the perfect asshole.

He'd walk along the platform of the market haggling with the sellers and calling them "jerk offs" if they charged too much. He hired a homeless guy to help him load his truck and gave him a wrinkled ten dollar bill, just enough to keep his wine habit alive for another day.

Once the truck was packed tight, he drove north on I-95 to his spot at the corner of Rising Sun and Cottman Avenue. He'd huckster the produce until dark, no matter how cold or hot the weather got, crouching in the back of the cab, putting fruit on a chain-linked scale, and ringing up the sales on his tiny cash register.

Morton Lapides was born to sell fruits and vegetables. It was in his DNA. The juice of blood oranges ran through his veins. He'd dream of skids of 90-pound crates of cantaloupes from Mexico, and smile as he loaded them onto a blue hand truck and cart them to his trailer where he would stack his merchandise perfectly, wasting no space or time, while other truckers would watch my father load his truck to find out his secret.

Rosalie and my father were living together even though he was still married to my mother. The two were not discreet, either. They celebrated shacking up, taking pictures of themselves making out and going to various vacation spots, while my mother was alone in a duplex apartment just three blocks down the street waiting for her husband to come home.

"Your father's never going to come out of the coma," Rosalie told me while I looked at my father making those popping sounds with his lips that grated on my nerves.

"How much time does he have left?"

"The doctor doesn't know for sure," Rosalie said while tears poured down her cheeks.

As I watched her cry, I wondered if they were crocodile tears and not from a genuine loss. Was she happy that my father was dying? Could she secretly be planning a financial windfall after he excluded me from his will and have her as the primary beneficiary?

"He wanted to talk to you," she said, "but he was too afraid that you might get angry."

Rosalie rubbed me the wrong way, but I didn't make a scene. I bided my time until I could be alone with my father and, perhaps, make peace with him before he died.

He had a terrible childhood, an alcoholic father and a mother so frugal that she bought him clothes two sizes too big. When Rosalie saw him alone in the truck, not only did she see a wounded soul with a bad marriage, but also a man who needed love and attention.

She swooped in like a barracuda. She went to Mort's produce truck every day and stayed there for hours. She brought him pots of beef stew, baked beans, and homemade potato perogies. She soon became a full-time employee and the customers mistook her for Mort's wife. She gave him pleasure while he gave her the daddy figure that she lacked.

Rosalie managed his business, bought him clothes, clipped his nose hairs, and soaked the stains out of his dentures with Polident. I understood that my lonely father needed someone, and that my mother was not the most loving person. I only wished that he had left my mother the right way—gotten a divorce, and settled everything legally.

The closer my father got to Rosalie, the more I distanced from him. I didn't want to condone their reprehensible affair or be stuck in the middle between my parents.

"Do you want some homemade chocolate chip cookies?" a woman with a big white cross around her neck asked.

She held a King James Bible under her right arm and touched my shoulder with her left hand. She recited passages from the scripture, something from Zechariah, "Not by might, nor by power, but by my spirit, saith the Lord of hosts," but I was too busy trying to figure out everything that was happening to me that day to appreciate it. Her religious support and chocolate chip cookies were the last things I needed.

"You know," she said, "your father's going to live forever. He found Jesus and he's going to be up there right next to him."

She looked to the heavens way too long. All I could see were the water stains on the ceiling.

"I'm praying to Jesus for your salvation. Kneel and recite a passage with me," she invited, attempting to pull me down to the floor.

"No!" I snarled, removing her hand from my shoulder. "I'm Jewish and I don't feel comfortable saying Christian prayers."

"I pray with Jews all the time," a smiling tall man named Ed interrupted. "Everyone can pray to Jesus."

He gave me a pretty intense back rub and squeezed my neck until I heard something crack.

"Come over to the church on Sunday," he said. "We're having a barbecue after the service and rides for the kids."

"I'm Jewish," I kept repeating to Ed. "I don't go to Christian churches."

"That's okay," he said. "Your Dad was Jewish and he loved our church. In fact, he was an usher; used to pass out the collection baskets."

I didn't want to offend any of these people even though they were offensive to me. They assumed that I needed salvation, that my soul was in jeopardy, but being a member of their congregation was not what I wanted.

One rather portly woman approached and pulled me close to her breast. Another held my hand and a few other people in the room offered bibles and rides to the church on Sunday if I didn't have one.

The room began to close in on me and I loosened my collar. The windows were shut and the heat turned up and so I was sweating like a pig. The TV was showing reruns of *Leave it to Beaver* without the sound. As the night wore on, I could see my father's comatose body slowly melting away with sudsy bubbles gushing out of the sides of his mouth.

I wanted to make amends with my dying father, but it was impossible. I couldn't get close enough to touch his hand or to feel his cold forehead because of all the hovering people vying for my conversion. It felt like yesterday when he was vibrant and alive and I couldn't wait till he got home so I could rub his bald head. I would grab my Richie Ashburn glove and toss a baseball in the backyard. He would crouch down in a catcher's stance and I would throw him a fastball. He always seem distracted, though. Like he was thinking about how many boxes of lettuce he needed for the store or other pressing things like the cost of a new transmission for his Ford Bronco.

I remembered the time he took me to Connie Mack Stadium on Lehigh Avenue in the early 60s. We drove there in his old ocean blue Cadillac with the big fins on the back. We saw the Chicago Cubs play the Phillies that night, and watched Ernie Banks smack a homer over the Coca-Cola sign in left field. Baseball was never so vivid and the grass field was never so green as that day my father took me to a game.

So many of Mort's stories ran through my head as I sat in the chair surrounded by strangers. That crazed juvenile delinquent who jumped on his car when he drove past the Daniel Boone School. The night in North Philly when a big guy sucker-punched him as he got out of his car to mail a letter. The story of the co-worker who accidentally severed his arm in heavy machinery. My father, thinking fast, threw his coat over the severed arm, stopped the bleeding, and saved the man's life.

As he lay dying in the family room of a narrow row house with pictures of strangers on the wall, he seemed anything but heroic. I thought of how rotten that dying man was. How undeserving of my love and time. I didn't want to feel the hatred. I wanted to think of him as a cute little boy growing up in the brutal winter of Northeastern Pennsylvania so I wouldn't have to despise him. I tried to remember the moments that he was kind and loving but they were too few and far between. Instead, I clenched my teeth and waited for the man who was called my father to turn into ashes and to be poured into a cremation urn.

I don't know how long I stayed in that house. I don't remember all the people that came up to me and said how wonderful my father was. They were people that my father knew, but they would always be strangers to me.

The strangers didn't care about how I felt and what I needed; they selfishly wanted to dip me into holy water and cleanse my spirit so they would have a better standing in heaven. They wanted me to carry a cross up the hill and rise from the dead or something equally painful. I only wanted to see my father in quiet and without all this unnecessary distraction. I didn't want to be saved or become Born Again. I just wanted to be alone with my dying father.

When I realized that I would never get that opportunity, I waited for the strangers to huddle in the kitchen, and then I bolted for the front door. I ran away like I was running from a scary nightmare. The first thing I did when I got home was to turn on the TV and raise the volume so I couldn't hear the angry voices in my head. For Chrissakes, my father was dying, yet the only thing I could think about was how his friends annoyed me.

I got down on my knees and prayed. I prayed to God to take away all the pain that my father and his friends inflicted on me.

I didn't pray the way the strangers wanted me to pray, to their God, but I prayed to the one God that I grew up with. He was the God that I believed could hear me even when I was only thinking. He was the one that I knew wouldn't hurt me.

He was the only father I trusted.

The Street of My Childhood

It was like a hurricane hit my childhood. The once immaculate neighborhood where I grew up was now dilapidated and rundown. Trash cans rolled past me and garbage swirled around this once proud neighborhood. There were broken chunks of cement in the sidewalks and torn up driveways. No little kids were riding bikes or laughing on the stoops. The front lawns grew high with weeds, abandoned cars with missing tires were hoisted up on jacks as a symbol of the city's decay.

My stoop was still there, though, as if it had survived the apocalypse. The house number hung loosely on one nail from the front bricks of the duplex where I lived, number 1023. I could see myself as a little kid waiting for Mister Softee to come around the corner with loose change stuck to my hands. I wore cut-off jeans then with my bony knees sticking out, a white T-shirt and a pair of Converse high-tops rounded out my summer wardrobe. I raced to the ice-cream truck on a hot summer day with all my friends—Donnie, Steve, and Ernie. "The last one there is a punk!" Ernie yelled. I didn't care about being a punk. I just wanted to get to the Mister Softee truck before it went to the next street or ran out of ice cream.

"Let me have a vanilla cone dipped in chocolate with sprinkles." I hollered up to the man with the white sailor's cap behind the window. I had to get the rainbow sprinkles. It made the ice-cream cone a masterpiece, a supremely flavorful treat.

Soon, I became transfixed in a sugary stupor, licking my

cone and hearing the noise from the cars, the baby cries, dogs barking in backyards, and my friends chattering in my ear. I bit into that crispy cone despite my teeth aching from the cold. The numbness at the roof of my mouth made my eyes tear with joy and pain.

In my mind, I could see myself sitting on the curb of my old street with an ice-cream cone dripping between my scuffed-up sneakers. I looked at the tire tracks and grease spills splattered on the street reminiscent of a Jackson Pollock painting. All those voices of my youth were in it. I could see Steve sitting on the curb coughing up a bunch of phlegm from his pleurisy. I could see Ernie with his shaky hands, always trembling from his nervous condition. Donnie, with his bushy hair and pot belly, swinging a fungo bat from his front lawn while imploring us to play a game.

I delivered newspapers on this street before the sun rose, folded and tossed them at the doorsteps, making sure they didn't come apart when they hit the ground. I still remember the smell of those freshly printed papers with the print ink tattooed to my palms. I still recalled the two old ladies who sat on the sofa at 1017 when I collected newspaper money. I could see right up their sundresses as they chain-smoked cigarettes and watched TV with their legs shamelessly spread.

The sound of my father's truck still rings in my ears. Whenever he came home, he took off a few branches as he turned the corner, parking close to the curb, the engine turning off with a clap and shudder. Steve's dad, a pharmacist, had a crimson Buick LeSabre parked proudly out front. Ernie's dad laid carpets for a living, and he had a van with his name on it. The man who delivered Tastykakes parked his truck near the corner where the fireplug was, but somehow never got a ticket. My next-door neighbor's car was the best. She had a Mustang convertible with an eight-track player. I could still hear Tommy James and the Shondells playing on her car stereo. I always thought it was so cool how the top slowly folded down on a summer day as if powered by the sun.

We used to peddle our Stingray bikes up and down our block, and watched with envy those kids who had gas-powered mini-bikes that puffed out a trail of black smoke as they blew by us. During the winter months, we got out our Radio Flyers from the garage and sledded down a steep hill a couple of blocks from our house. The snow was falling around us. We were cold with runny noses but kept going up and down the hill until our mothers called us in for a lunch of grilled cheese and tomato soup.

On Saturday, I'd wake up earlier than anyone. I couldn't wait to throw a pinkie ball against the steps. I had the street to myself until a couple of German Shepherds attacked me from behind. The dogs knocked me to the ground and ripped apart my clothes. I blacked out for a few seconds and, when I awoke, they were gone like two thieves in the night. My face was gouged, and a big welt grew over my right eye. Back then, my doctor made a house call and gave me stitches right on the spot.

It was our street back then—wild dogs, cars, sleds and all. It was where our whole world happened, where our hearts beat fast, and our legs pumped like pistons with so much energy that we thought we'd explode. It was where we could get away from the watchful eyes of our parents and just be kids with all our crude imperfections.

When we played touch football in the street, we were always annoyed at the cars who temporarily interrupted our games. We thought we owned the street and felt offended that someone was trespassing. We were only puny city kids, but we acted like we had the strength of grown men, giving evil eyes and flipping the bird to whoever passed, knowing full well that if they had stopped and gotten out of their cars, we would run like hell.

Mandy Pinkerman lived across from me with the big white and gray awning over her front door. I could almost picture her sitting outside in her Madras shorts with her long tan legs folded on the top step. Even though her parents were divorced, it didn't seem to affect her. She always had friends, and there was one guy who looked like he was in college who used to lay on the grass playing with her long brown hair and making her giggle.

Back then, I had a thing for Mandy. I paid a little runt twenty cents to put a letter in the mail slot of her screen door. It was a love letter with only a few words inside a big red crayon heart. I told her she was too beautiful to describe, but the truth was, I didn't have enough words at my disposal to tell her how I felt.

I was too afraid to sign my name on the letter, so I put my initials on opposite ends of the paper hoping that eventually she could decipher it. There was a part of me that hoped that she would never discover my identity; because love unconsummated was perhaps the best kind of love.

Her attitude had changed once she read the note. For some reason, she knew who was dumb enough to do such a thing, and you can't trick girls that easily. So, instead of saying hello with a friendly smile, she gave me a funny look like I was a stupid little creep who wrote pervy letters to pretty girls because I was too afraid to talk to them.

After that, my interest in Mandy fell off. I realized that it was a childish infatuation and that I should look for girls my age who weren't so pretty and didn't have boyfriends who went to college. I eventually discovered that there were girls who liked me and that I didn't have to pine over the ones out of my league.

It didn't take long until I found one. I ran into a girl from my homeroom named Cherry Templeton at the ice-skating rink. I accidentally knocked her to the ice one Friday night, helped her up, and we started to flirt. She had short blonde hair like Twiggy and wore a pink parka with white mittens. After doing several laps around the rink, we went to the Tarken Playground and sat on one of those steel merry-go-rounds for little kids. We sang "Build Me Up Buttercup" together and that's when I planted my first kiss.

Soon after, we went steady. I'd meet her at her corner duplex under a flight of stairs. She was not as beautiful as Mandy, but I could talk to her about anything and trusted her with my heart. I realized back then that it was the connection that mattered and not the way a girl looked.

"Build Me Up Buttercup" kept playing in my head as I kissed Cherry again and again under the stairs. Back then, a kiss meant that we had a commitment so I had to get her a ring. I picked up a plastic ring for fifteen cents at a variety store. The value of the ring was worth more than the few pennies I paid. Holding it in my little hands, it felt more valuable than a diamond ring that you bought from a jewelry store.

The next day, I kissed Cherry again. This time, I tried to put my heart into it and make it unforgettable. Then I slipped the ring on her finger as I heard a marching band playing in my head with clashing symbols. She smiled with her pale, cracked lips and her blue eyes glistened like shining stars. She returned the kiss, and she put her head on my chest as we promised our love forever.

A couple of days later, I went to see Cherry and her mother answered the door. She was none too happy. Without saying more than a few words, she handed me back the ring and gave me a disapproving look like I was some pervert trying to corrupt her daughter.

"Cherry's too young to have a ring from a boy," she said, and abruptly slammed the door in my face.

I remember asking myself, *how could she do that to us?* Love was so rare, and when one is lucky enough to find it, a door shouldn't be slammed on it. I stood at Cherry's house for a few minutes, just staring at the ring of rejection. I felt I wasn't good enough for Cherry. One day, I was the happiest kid on the block, feeling as lucky as anybody, then the next day my heart was broken and my dreams blown to smithereens.

The street of my memories had its share of ups and downs. I loved my friends, even the German Shepherds, and especially my neighbor who drove me in her Ford Mustang with the top down. I loved when Henry, the neighborhood hippie, would play Beatles songs in the driveway like "Michelle" and "Ticket to Ride." I loved when I thought about how lucky I was after a summer rain when the sun came out and everything in the street smelled so fresh and sweet.

Even at an early age, I knew that the excitement and wonder on my street was temporary. Steve's troubled lungs would ebb and flow with the humidity and the cold. My infatuation with certain girls would seem to peak with the seasons. Our Philly sports teams would win some and then go into the dumpster. Mister Softee would come to our block one day and another day we'd never hear that sweet jingle. My mother grew older with age spots that insidiously appeared on her face and arms. My father rarely came home, and the sound of his truck's grinding gears slowly diminished with time. A neighborhood that was once beautiful and full of life would gradually fall apart. But my childhood memories never seem to go away, no matter how old I get.

To Princess Lilly

I sat on Dad's brown leather recliner when I visited you. My teeth clenched as you uncurled my fingers, placed the newspaper in my hand and demanded that I read every section of the Sunday Philadelphia Inquirer.

You thought the newspaper would make me a more informed human being. Nobody informed you that your rational brain hadn't worked in years. You were foggy and confused from all the dopamine swishing around in your head. You saw dancing demons on the ceiling and you kept saying to me:

Lean back, don't crouch over.
Sit up in the chair.
Don't walk like that.

You succeeded in making me crazy. I walked out of the house naked one day just like you did. My poor wife had to notify the police that I was headed for the Ben Franklin Bridge; the same bridge you planned to jump off. I wanted to be free of the voices in my head and have the cold river wash away all the memories of you.

But I stayed alive despite everything.

I fought and fought. I resisted you pushing my shoulders against the chair. You straightened my legs but I turned them out. I didn't let you control any part of my body because I knew what happened to my father when he gave in.

He died of a heart attack at fifty. The poor man didn't have a chance. The only way to get away from you was to find a nice peaceful place inside a coffin. By the time you got through with him, he didn't have a hair left on his head. His body wasn't even cold when you took off his ragged hairpiece and stuck it on my head.

"Leave it on. It looks good," you said with a crazy laugh.

You weren't going to make me wear a dead man's hairpiece. I yanked it off my head, pulled up the screen window and tossed it two stories below to the neighbor's Chinese vegetable garden. It landed right next to the radish patch, just above the green bell peppers. I hoped it would do some good there, certainly more productive than it would have been on my head.

You wanted me to cover my bare pate but you wore clothes with stains from Milk of Magnesia and cod liver oil. Your torn stockings hung down to your ankles revealing your hairy legs. Half the time you walked out of the house with no panties under your dress.

No wonder I never stopped crying.

I moved to Williamsburg, Brooklyn to get away from you. I hoped that the noise of the city could drown out the voices that you put in my head. I thought if I got married, I would somehow forget my past. My therapist told me to make strong boundaries, to limit the phone calls and visits. He upped the dosage of my anti-psychotic medication and gave me pills to numb the pain.

"Bizarre women say bizarre things," he said. "They bring you to a place that you don't want to go and if one of them happens to be your mother, you just might be the unluckiest person on earth. It won't matter if you love her or not, she'll never change; she'll never conform to what a normal mother should be. No matter how far away you move or how many drugs you take, there's no getting away from her, even when she lies lifeless on the cold linoleum floor."

I wish I could forget you.

The false teeth floating in a jar. The chipped porcelain sink. The old moldy plastic slipcovers on your sofa and chairs. Devil's food cake cracked and broken. An old piece of gefilte fish on a paper plate.

You forced me to say Kaddish for the dead over a burning Yahrzeit candle in the kitchen. The candle reminded you of your father who called you *Princess Lilly*. You loved sitting on his lap. You haven't stopped praying for his soul since the night he was crushed by a Broad Street train going southbound.

"Be careful," you kept telling me.

You had me believing that something tragic would happen every time I stepped out of the house.

But it was you who died on the cold linoleum floor in the kitchen. You greeted me with the stench of death. I expected you to be in the same pathetic state since my last visit three weeks ago. Instead you were lying there; face down, with the ants, roaches and flies that you so affectionately maintained.

Before calling the police, I walked through each room of your apartment. I opened every piece of mail. I looked at the photo album with pictures of me inside of my old Volkswagen Beetle and dad in his Army uniform standing in front of the Eiffel Tower. I leafed through your 1952 high school yearbook and was reminded of how beautiful you were and that you were once normal like everyone else. But then your world fell apart shortly after your father died. You graduated high school and you married a bald man that you never really loved, had a baby, and then you lost your mind, strapped to a table, hooked up to an electro-shock therapy machine and for the next forty years you would be a demented woman living on the second floor of a duplex, alone.

By the time I was out of diapers, I realized that you were insane and that I would never get the love and attention that I deserved. I hoped that you would change, stop talking to yourself and behave like a real mother. But I set the bar too high. You always disappointed me, made me angry and crazy.

Even in your rigor mortis, I couldn't cry for you. There were just too many painful memories to have a place for you in my heart. If only you had jumped off the Ben Franklin Bridge like you planned, maybe I would have felt at least a grain of sympathy.

As I waited for the police to arrive, I lit one of your Yahrzeit candles in the kitchen. As the black smoke spiraled in the air, with your body lying still and face down, I took a deep breath and repeated the words that you planted in my head.
Lean back, don't crouch over.
Sit up in the chair.
Don't walk like that.

Fall So Beautifully

For months, my father's 1982 black Ford pickup, with the colorful fruit basket stenciled on its doors, was parked on the side street, just off of Roosevelt Boulevard. Many of his customers walked by hoping that Mort was still there hawking his produce. He was their friend and the only person that they trusted buying their merchandise from, even though the fruit vendor a couple of streets down was a lot cheaper.

Mort, by nature, was a produce man, and so was his brother, his father, and grandfather. It was in his blood. He knew how sweet his red plums tasted even before he took a bite. He could tell you where the Granny Smith apples were grown, how his yellow corn was harvested, and what's the name of the farm that picked his Yukon Gold potatoes.

"Sitting on my ass," as he called it, per doctor's orders, was not the way he wanted to spend the last years of his life. He grew bored of walking back and forth from his bedroom to the living room to the kitchen while carting around his oxygen tank, wishing it was the steel blue hand truck that he pushed so many loads of iceberg lettuce. He couldn't stand being cooped up in a house, looking at silly game shows, simple-minded programs that he had no interest in watching. He believed that he should be climbing up on his truck's tailgate, selling produce, and bullshitting with his customers about the price of Spanish onions and the cost of Crenshaw melons.

The only time he felt alive was when he was on the back of

his Ford pick-up with the big wooden cap that he built himself. He needed to get out of the house, somehow, and stop wasting precious time.

"Screw the doctors," he said when I told him that he should stay home a couple more months to recuperate from the surgery following his latest setback.

"Take it easy, Dad," I said. "You just had a serious operation. Relax."

My father was a stubborn man, and also a born salesman. He could convince a cat to stop chasing a mouse. So, it didn't take much to persuade me to let him back on the truck.

"All I want to do," he pleaded, "is to sell my fruit and see my customers again. You can do all the heavy work."

His sallow, wrinkled face told me that being in the house all day was slowly killing him. No longer was he that strong, masculine man that I once admired. His shoulders drooped; folds of skin dangled from his neck. His once bright blue eyes were now bloodshot and watery with sorrow.

"Just this once, Dad, and if you feel exhausted, I'll take you right home. Agreed?"

He smiled with those yellowing dentures. His sweaty bald head shimmered from the kitchen's fluorescent lights. Even with his failing body, he still had some hope.

The next morning, I loaded the truck with produce at the South Philly market, and picked up my father who was waiting at the front door with his portable oxygen tank by his side. I folded up his walker and stuck it behind the back seat. When we hit a bump, he grimaced from the soreness in his chest but denied that anything was wrong.

"I'm fine! I'm fine! Don't worry, just drive," and shooed me with his hands.

Once at his prized location off the boulevard, I set up the produce display just as he would have liked it. When I stacked the oranges and apples in majestic pyramids, he gazed at my work in awe, almost identical to the way he had done it, so careful and precise.

He shuffled his feet while scraping the walker on the sidewalk, dragging his oxygen tank like a stubborn dog being pulled by a leash. Even with his frail body and failing heart, he kept pushing toward the truck as if he were on a sacred mission.

"Why didn't you tell me you could set up a truck by yourself? I would have given you more money," he said with a laugh and a hacking cough. "Go ahead, make some room up there for me."

He motioned for help, so I retrieved a stepstool and gave him my shoulder to balance on. After a few attempts, his skinny old legs found the strength to push onto the tailgate, and I handed him the oxygen tank. I made sure he held onto a box of bell peppers as he shuffled to the front corner of the truck where he could sit on a milk crate, the Harbison Dairy one, that he used for over forty years.

In a phlegmy voice, he shouted, "I want to wait on my customers!" as if calling to the produce Gods to make a miracle happen.

Like smoke signals sent up to the sky, his customers somehow got the message that their friend Mort was back and flocked to his fruit truck like hordes of religious believers, coming in pairs, clusters of three and four, as if they were going to hear the Sermon on the Mount.

"He's back!" one customer screamed.

Another said: "Finally! We missed you, Uncle Mort!"

"I can't believe it!" squawked the customer who always brought him homemade oatmeal cookies and lasagna.

Once situated at his rightful place on the truck, Mort knew how to get started: He turned on the transistor radio and extended its antennae. He rotated the knob with his gnarled fingers to his favorite station. The Phillies were in the fifth inning, playing at home against the Cincinnati Reds with Curt Schilling on the mound. The announcer's booming voices called the play by play with the same down-home enthusiasm that made him feel comfortable.

He touched the metal scale to see if he was dreaming. It hung from the roof of the truck with its big numerical face seemingly smiling at Mort, happy that he was back as well. He made sure that the arrow was pointing to zero so his customers would get an honest reading.

He knew that his life was on the truck. Mort was a produce man. His brother was one, and so was his father and grandfather. He didn't know anything else but to buy and huckster fruits and vegetables off the backend of a truck and to work long, hard hours with not a whole lot of financial reward except the relationships he developed.

"How are you, Mort?" asked his favorite customer. They were all his favorites. He never met one he didn't like.

He grabbed the Bosc pears in his shaky hands and leveled the scale so he could drop them in the scoop without them falling.

He kept smiling like it was his birthday and people were throwing him a party.

"That looks like two pounds. Put a couple more in," Dad said, "and we could make it an even three bucks."

Dad's hands shook as he took the money and awkwardly rung it up on his little manual register.

He was a different man when he was on the truck; a produce guru, a wise man that people revered. I don't know if it was his broad smile or just his charming personality. Whatever it was, if he said something was a bargain, they didn't dispute it. They dropped the grapes, tangerines or whatever they had into a plastic bag and hoisted it up on the scale. They told him about their love lives, their children away at college. They told him things that most professional counselors didn't hear in their fancy offices.

Another customer handed Mort a few more peaches. The scale topped three-and-a-quarter pounds, but he never was a stickler.

"Three pounds right on the nose," he smiled to the man who gladly handed him a five dollar bill and waited for the change.

Mort turned to me with his rheumy eyes and congested lungs, "See, son. That's how you do it." And with that, he grabbed his chest at the area of the heart and started to pant like a thirsty dog. He grimaced in pain and tried to grab something in his pants pocket.

"Are you okay, Dad?"

He didn't answer as I watched him sway forward, sideways, then backward, pulling down the stack of plastic bags and the hanging scale with him. He fell into several bushel baskets of large, beefsteak tomatoes. He lay on his back surrounded in the truck with all the fruits and vegetables that meant so much to him. It wasn't just produce. They were his children—the greens, reds, and the yellows that gathered around him for one final time.

I never saw anyone fall so beautifully. Dad's head gently burst open several of the tomatoes that slowly oozed out their savory liquid. He lay there with his bluish chapped lips spread into a broad smile. Tomatoes were his favorite food. He would eat a ripe tomato by itself, sprinkle some salt on it, and bite into it like it was a juicy filet mignon.

I watched him lay on the tomatoes for a few seconds until I called 911. I didn't get upset or panic when he stopped breathing, nor did all of his favorite customers who gathered around their huckstering prince. Together we watched, taking a mental picture of the man that we loved and respected. We wanted to remember Mort in the back of his truck with all his fruits and vegetables because that's how a produce man was supposed to die.

The Spirit of the Wooden Box

It took me until I was sixty to appreciate you. It's a shame that you had to die before I could acknowledge your impact on my life. Too bad you're in a wooden box now in the living room, all ashes, just a spirit of burnt remains.

Now that you're dead, I can barely hear your cries. There's no anger. No unmet needs or disappointments. No crazy garbled words or high heels whizzing past my forehead through a bay window and falling onto the street. No telling me to sit up straight in a chair or to read the *Home and Garden* section of the Sunday paper or chastising me for wearing the color blue in the house. Just your pure memory lingers, the good overriding the bad. The essence of your perfect version.

Every time I look at the wooden box that sits on the drawing table, I hear a quiet voice, no longer screaming with tears streaming down your face. No longer talking in riddles, playing the victim, complaining about things that no one cared about or even understood.

There is only silence without breath. Your quiet spirit hovers in and around the wooden box as I prepare your favorite dinner: pasta in red sauce, a baguette, a bottle of Chianti. Your spirit keeps me company, my ally, and my honored guest. When I interact with the insurance adjuster, you help me calculate the numbers. When I inhale my Albuterol through a nebulizer, you encourage me to take a deeper breath. I can finally tolerate being close to you. No longer do

I have to create distance or drink myself to sleep to get you out of my head.

The wooden box has a Yahrzeit candle burning above it with a trail of black smoke rising to the ceiling. Whenever I see that candle flame flicker, I think of you praying for my deceased father over the kitchen sink. I watched your trembling hands clutch a prayer book, your parched lips muttering a chant in Hebrew, your eyes closed while rocking back and forth like you were at the Western Wall of Jerusalem.

Next to the burning candle is the image of you as a teenager, posing on a stoop with long brown hair, wearing a high school letter on your sweater, and resembling a young Elizabeth Taylor with a closed-lip smile. You were surprisingly beautiful then, seemingly had the world at your fingertips with a clear plan about your future. You wanted to write brilliant poetry and short stories that would make people see the world from a more compassionate place. Then you met a man, convinced yourself that you loved him, had a baby, and then lost your mind. The photo makes me think of what might have been if you hadn't gotten married and settled for a muted life, taking care of a man who never encouraged you to follow your dreams.

"You don't have to feel sorry for me or worry anymore," your spirit whispers.

"I can't help it," I say. "You seemed so vulnerable, barely five-foot tall, and I feared that people would take advantage of you."

But then I realized that you were far from incapable of taking care of yourself. You launched Coke bottles at a bully across the street that teased you for the way you dressed. You threatened to break a car window with my Louisville Slugger when a neighborhood boy walked on your flowerbed. Despite your diminutive size, you were as fearless as a pit bull.

Your spirit whispers to me not to betray myself or to deny who I am.

"Don't question your intuition," you say. "Live the kind of life that you dream about. I weighed myself down with fear and never listened to my inner voice, but you can rise above it."

I stand motionless, lightheaded with nostalgia. I see you clipping my mittens to my coat sleeves and opening up a can of Campbell's Tomato Soup to go with the grilled cheese sandwich browning on the skillet. I see you push me down a snowy hill in a red Flexible Flyer, watching me until I make it safely to the bottom. You take pictures of me in the swimming pool while riding a walrus float, sliding into third base under a tag at a Little League baseball game, and in my glen plaid bar mitzvah suit standing awkwardly right after I became a man. With your Kodak camera, you captured all my sacred events and then neatly pasted those developed photographs into an album, chronicling my life's story with your stamp of approval.

I stand in front of the wooden box, now, acknowledging all the things that you did for me, feeling guilty that I never returned the favor. I always focused on your insanity, never on the person behind the crazy talk.

"I wish I could do my childhood over," I tell the spirit of the wooden box.

"It's not about me. It's about you," the spirit answers.

I nod my head. I tap lightly on the wooden box. The Yahrzeit candle flickers with a beautiful orange flame that reminds me that you are still here.

Finding My Father

My bones feel creaky and brittle; there's a mild pain in my lower back that hurts whenever I take a deep breath. I need to get out of town, to get away from everything. I don't want to tell anyone—family, friends or co-workers. Just drive as far as my car can take me. I'm itchy for a new experience, anything to make me feel different and to take the pain away.

So, I get in my rundown Mazda, and I drive up the coast, searching for a sign, a message, or an experience that could help me find my direction. My father had always been my friend and mentor. He always supported me. He encouraged me like a good counselor. He was the one that I went to when I felt stuck. Now I'm stuck, and he's gone.

He always said the right things. They were simple words, but he told them generously, from a place that was real and sincere. When I pined for a woman and didn't think I would ever find one, he told me that there was a "lid for every pot." When I was in the hospital suffering from pneumonia, hooked up to an IV and despondent, he told me that at least I didn't have cancer. They were silly comments, some may even consider them to be insensitive, but you had to know my father. The things that he said came from the right place. He knew how to make me feel better.

Heading north to the Bay Area from my home in Santa Cruz, I get on Route 1 and drive. A country song on the radio reminds me of him. He liked singers like Merle Haggard and

Johnny Cash who had a chip on their shoulders. He called them *down-to-earth* people. "These guys don't bullshit you," he said. "They speak the truth."

My father was a simple and unpretentious man. He sold fruits and vegetables, a profession handed down by his father. If you knew him, you'd call him a blue-collar guy, a hard worker who wasn't afraid to get his hands dirty. He always put in a good day's work, coming home each night with scuffed boots and dirty work shirts. He labored long and hard for many years.

He wanted me to have a more comfortable life, one where I wouldn't have to wake up early in the morning and load a truck with fruits and vegetables. He wanted something better for me, not to labor so many hours and wreck my body lifting heavy boxes of produce.

Passing the citrus fields and avocado farms reminds me of him. I see his large hands and stubby fingers put a 100-pound bag of potatoes on his back. He dumps the potatoes into a display bin and removes the bad ones without using gloves. I see him putting a couple of wooden crates of cantaloupes on his handcart and wheeling it to the cooler. He weighs a hand of bananas on a hanging scale. He smiles at a customer with his thick lips and a mouth full of false teeth. He tells the customer to throw in another banana or two to make it three pounds. He never charged extra when it went over.

I'm driving north because I want to see the redwood trees with centuries of history that could put my life in perspective. I want to be in the middle of the Muir Woods and surround myself with nature, lose my melancholy, and feel strong again.

An image of my father pushing me on a swing comes to me as I reach my destination. He helps me up the slide and makes a funny whistle when I slide down. He holds my rump when I climb the monkey bars so I don't fall, and teaches me how to bounce a basketball without losing the dribble. We laugh and hug each other. He comforts me when I bruise my knee. He reminds me to be kind to other children and to respect adults.

Thinking of him makes me feel good. When I'm with him,

everything feels the way it should be, and nothing will ever change. Time will stand still, and I will never grow old. He will live forever.

Walking along the wooden pathway of the Muir Woods, I see luscious green plants, tiny animals, insects, and hear the tapping sounds of woodpeckers. Nature is arranged so perfectly, just like my father arranged his fruit truck with his merchandise, no space wasted, things put where they are supposed to go.

I breathe in the misty, fresh air and then sigh it all out.

Polaroid pictures of my father holding me as a baby flash in my head. He held me tight, not wanting me to fall. He looked at me like he was looking at a miracle. His eyes watered with happiness as his emotions ran high. He whispered that he would always take care of me no matter how old I got.

He'd let go and allow me to walk at my own speed. He didn't push or pull me as some parents might do. He didn't try to control my movements but let me explore life at my own pace. When he did grip my hand, it made me feel secure and loved.

Right now, I'm trying not to cry. If my father were here, he would tell me to let it all out. He was very masculine, but he believed that it was okay for a man to cry. He cried at his brother's funeral, at my mother's struggle with mental illness, and the many other sad events in our lives. Whenever he got upset, his bald head turned red, his glasses fogged, and then he carefully cleaned them with a tissue in order to see. It was helpful to watch him cry. It made me not be so afraid of feelings.

I cry because I long for him to be breathing and his blood circulating through his body. He squeezes my shoulders when he hugs. I sit on his lap as a kid, and he bounces me up and down on his knee. I can't stop feeling dizzy.

Weak and vulnerable, I walk slowly through the woods. It will soon be my time to stop living. It might be tomorrow or next week, or sometime in the distant future, I don't know. I'll be dead and gone, and my kids will go through the same melancholy journey. *Why did he leave me so suddenly? I should have taken better care of him or encouraged him to see the doctor.*

I'm trying to stop crying.

My legs feel shaky like I'm about to fall. My father holds me upright so I can stand. He taught me to walk, to ride a bike, and to drive a car. He taught me things that nobody else would. He didn't yell at me when I made mistakes but just told me to keep trying.

The sunlight splinters through the tall trees making the spiderwebs look like beautiful kaleidoscopes of color. I lose myself in the whistling wrens, the blue jay songs, owls hooting, scurrying wood mice, crayfish in the stream, snowy egrets with skinny legs, and the river otters dipping and diving in splashing water.

Standing beside the tall trees with their massive bark, I find myself experiencing their unspoken wisdom. The trees survived far worse times than I have. Their power and history far outweigh mine. I dig my heels into the earth to take root. Closing my eyes, I pause. I imagine I'm one of them, if just for an instant.

My father touches my shoulder, again. He is silent in his strength. He communicates to me without words, confirming that everything is all right. Death comes and goes. I have to remember not to try to control it, but to embrace change.

As I walk further, my father is young again. He is not hooked up to a respirator. He is no longer on life support gasping for air and barely living. He is fully conscious, breathing freely, functioning without any help from nurses or doctors. There is no longer the need for a morphine drip to ease the pain. He is happy again. He smiles at me for the longest time and slowly dissolves into the cool forest mist, leaving behind the working man's gritty odor that once defined him.

My energy has come back. The pain in my lower back seems to have disappeared. The palette of nature's colors in Muir Woods appears more beautiful and vibrant now. With each step, I feel more in harmony with the way things are.

I call my wife to tell her where I am and that I'm on the way home. She informs me that my son is out with his friends and that my daughter is in her room finishing a term paper. My wife says that there's some stew cooking in the Crockpot and would I please pick up some French bread on the way home.

The oyster and turkey tail mushrooms are below my feet on the forest floor. The insects, spiders, squirrels, and chipmunks move around me as the woods engulf me with their natural healing power. I forget my fears, my loss, and have a renewed sense of well-being.

The darkening sky signals me to make my way quickly back to the car. It gets windy, and the leaves swirl around me. Looking up at the tall trees for one last time, they seem to be reaching for the heavens.

About the Author

Mark Tulin's formative years were spent in Philadelphia playing baseball and getting into mischief with his friends. He parlayed his experiences growing up in a dysfunctional family to become a successful marriage and family therapist. Once he retired and relocated to California, his interest in creative writing flourished. His stories have appeared in anthologies, journals, and podcasts. He has published in *Page & Spine*, *Cabinet of the Heed*, and *Fiction on the Web*, among others. His poetry chapbook, *Magical Yogis*, was published by Prolific Press in 2017, and his poetry collection, *Awkward Grace*, was published by Kelsay Press in 2019. Follow Mark at www.crowonthewire.com.

Lightning Source UK Ltd.
Milton Keynes UK
UKHW010959290820
369029UK00001B/190